"You can't mean you think I'm a witch!"

Inary said.

Ford shrugged. "What you are, you are. It has nothing to do with what I think. Whether you accept it or not, you have power. Latent, at the moment, but shining clearly enough to be seen by anyone who has the ability. Power attracts power, Inary, including those who covet yours."

"I don't believe a word of this," Inary said coldly.

"Then you face more danger than either of us can cope with."

"But I don't have any power!" she cried. "And I don't want any."

"The choice isn't yours. You can't give power away, but those who covet what you have can subvert you and use your power for their own selfish purposes."

"And how do you know all this—this esoteric mumbo jumbo?"

When Ford spoke again, his tone was somber. "I know because I have powers, too...."

Dear Reader,

Once again, we're here to chill you and thrill you with two more Shadows titles. And I think you're going to enjoy both these books—especially if you read them with the lights off and a summer breeze wafting through the window to shiver along your skin.

Carla Cassidy's *Heart of the Beast* is an irresistible exploration of the nature of man—and the nature of the beasts. Things are not quite what they seem in this book. Or maybe they are. You'll have to decide for yourself.

Jane Toombs once again proves herself mistress of the Gothic with *Dark Enchantment*. After reading this book, you'll never look at your neighbor in quite the same way again!

In months to come, look for more terrific Shadows novels coming your way from authors like Barbara Faith, Lee Karr and many more "mistresses of the macabre."

Enjoy!

Leslie Wainger
Senior Editor and Editorial Coodinator

JANE TOOMBS

DARK ENCHANTMENT

▼ SILHOUETTE® Shadows™

Published by Silhouette Books New York

America's Publisher of Contemporary Romance

SILHOUETTE BOOKS
300 East 42nd St., New York, N.Y. 10017

DARK ENCHANTMENT

Copyright © 1993 by Jane Toombs

ISBN: 0-373-27012-7

First Silhouette Books printing July 1993

All the characters in this book have no existence outside the imagination of the author and have no relation whatsoever to anyone bearing the same name or names. They are not even distantly inspired by any individual known or unknown to the author, and all incidents are pure invention.

® and ™:Trademarks used with authorization. Trademarks indicated with ® are registered in the United States Patent and Trademark Office, the Canada Trade Mark Office and in other countries.

Printed in the U.S.A.

JANE TOOMBS

believes that a touch of the mysterious adds spice to a romance. Her childhood fascination with stories about shape changers such as vampires, werewolves and shamans never faded, leading to her present interest in supernatural influences, not only in Gothic romances but in the early cultures of all peoples.

A Californian transplanted to New York, Jane and her writer husband live in the shadow of Storm King Mountain.

CHAPTER ONE

Almost there, Inary Cameron told herself. I'll reach the house well before dark and then I'll be safe.

White clouds scudded across the lowering sun, making an alternate shadow-light pattern across the blacktop. The late March sun was warm, but her car windows were rolled up against the cold wind as spring dragged reluctant feet into Michigan's Upper Peninsula.

Woods, large stands of second growth, lined the state highway as she sped toward Lake Superior. The evergreens, maples and oaks had grown tall in the hundred years since the logging days. From time to time she caught a glimpse of unmelted snow between the trees where the sun didn't reach.

Sparse towns straggled along the road occasionally but the overwhelming impression was of wilderness. She passed Norwich, the last village before the turnoff to the old house. Now the girth of the trees increased; virgin timber the loggers had missed grew near the lake.

In California she'd envisioned this white pine forest, the thickness of ancient trees hiding her, the worn, defiant gray of the old house barring intruders, the big lake repelling the incursion of evil. Here, no High Sierra peaks stared down, constantly watching, knowing all. Aunt Inary's house on Lake Superior, nestled in the cold virgin forest, was a longed-for sanctuary.

She could still remember their last meeting and the chill in her aunt's voice when she'd told her never to come to the house again. Despite this, Aunt Inary had left the old place to her when she died, and thank God she had. But she still wondered what had made her aunt change her mind.

Inary spotted the No Trespassing sign, to her surprise a new one, not the old, faded, barely legible sign of her childhood. Turning her car to the left, she eased into a narrow, rutted lane. Pines crowded the car from both sides as she crept along the sandy drive. Underbrush scraped the sides, causing the two cats in the back seat to make restless noises.

"Just a few minutes more," she assured them.

Then Aunt Inary's house rose before her. *Her* house, really, if she could get used to the idea. She stopped the car, rolled down the window and inhaled the aromatic scent of the pines as she gazed lovingly at the old place. "A rambling three-story monstrosity," her father had always called it. "A Victorian white elephant in a land beyond the moon."

Perhaps that was why, when her aunt died last Christmas, she'd left the house to her niece rather than her brother. They were the only surviving relatives.

"Sell it!" her father had advised when he heard what she'd inherited. "You'll never live in that godforsaken spot. You won't get a fortune for the old wreck, but there should be enough for a nice little condo in a decent climate."

But she hadn't even tried to sell it. Neither had she been in any hurry to claim her heritage, preferring the false warmth and the fool's gold of California. Until the dark whispers began.....

Inary shook her head and focused her attention on the house. She'd left danger behind her; she wouldn't think of the past. The old place looked much as she remembered. She'd always loved the look of the three-sided tower over the porch held up by spindly columns, seemingly too frail to bear the weight. The porch was odd-shaped because of the tower overhang, the massive oak front door it protected incongruous between the delicate columns.

Another outcropping, a small octagonal affair consisting mostly of windows, sat on the main roof like a too-small hat. Actually it was a skylight to illuminate the attic. Big maples to the sides and back of the house thrust bare branches higher than the chimneys while a tall mountain ash grew in front.

One of the cats set up a yowl, reminding her they'd been cooped up far too long. She opened the door, slid out and thrust the back of the seat forward. Reaching in, she lifted the heavy cat carrier with both hands.

"You guys eat too much, you know?" she muttered.

Inary set the carrier on the porch while she fumbled in her bag for the key, shivering in the chilly lake breeze. She tried the door in a reflex action before inserting the key and drew in her breath in surprise when the knob turned in her hand. Not locked? Cautiously she eased the door open and peered inside before entering. She expected the musty smell of disuse, but a faint fragrance of roses drifted to meet her, making her recall her aunt's rose-petal sachets.

Gilgamesh complained loudly, and she lifted the carrier again, putting it down in the entry while she closed the door, relishing the cozy warmth of the house. As soon as she unfastened the carrier door, Gilgamesh, a short-haired gray cat with a white chest, pushed out to investigate, and long-haired black Enkidu lurched clumsily after him.

Picking up Enkidu, she called, "Is someone in the house?"

There was no answer. She shrugged, determined not to let herself be frightened by an unlocked door, and, still carrying the cat, Inary passed through the foyer where steep, winding stairs led to the second story. She raised her eyebrows at the birch log fire in the brick fireplace of the living room.

"Who's here?" she called.

Again no answer. The lawyer who'd written her about her inheritance—the first she'd heard of Aunt Inary's death—had mentioned the house was being looked after. Did that mean keeping a fire lit when there was central heat? She headed for the kitchen at the back of the house, wondering if there'd be a fire in the black wood stove, too.

There was. The kitchen itself was spotless—no dust, no mouse droppings. Soap and a sponge sat on a countertop next to the old sink. She crossed to the eating area, noting that the benches were tucked neatly under the overhang of the well-scrubbed pine table. The back door wasn't locked either, so she clicked the lock into place.

Surely the welcoming fires couldn't be for her, because she'd let no one know she was coming. She glanced into the partial basement where the furnace, hot-water heater and oil-storage tank took up all the space, then went on to the dining room her aunt used as a den, finding it as neat as the other rooms. As she completed the circle back to the foyer, Gilgamesh called from somewhere above, and she started up the stairs.

The three bedrooms were empty except for the furniture. Enkidu squirmed in her arms and she put him down on the patchwork quilt covering the four-poster bed in her aunt's old room, the room with the three-sided tower. She knew the bed had been made up recently because the sheets smelled fresh. In the bathroom the fixtures gleamed and unused towels hung neatly from the racks.

Was someone staying here? The house didn't have a lived-in look, though—everything was too neat, too clean. Ready but not yet in use. Evidently the lawyer had hired an excellent caretaker, except for the fact that the house had been left unlocked. The caretaker couldn't be around since there'd been no car outside, and it was a long walk into town. Aunt Inary had had no neighbors nearby because she owned Agate Point and its surrounding acreage and refused to sell to anyone.

I own the point now, Inary thought dazedly. I own the house and all the land. Her mind was fuzzy, not working well—too many days on the road and restless nights in motels. She desperately needed to sleep. But not until she was certain no one was in the house—she hadn't looked in the attic yet.

Gilgamesh had been trailing her from room to room, but when she opened the door to the attic and started up the steps, he stayed behind. Inary blinked when she came to the top of the stairs and saw how clean the attic was. Hadn't the place once been cluttered with trunks and boxes?

Returning to the first floor, she found both cats waiting in the entry. Enkidu uttered an inquiring meow that she'd learned meant, "I can't find a sandbox—when are you going to let me outside?"

She opened the front door for them and unloaded the car while they took care of their needs. By the time she had everything piled in the entry, they were ready to come inside again. Enkidu's lurching gait tugged at her heart but the veterinarian who'd treated his amputated paw had warned against pampering him.

After locking the front door, she fed the cats in the kitchen, then examined the cupboards. Fully stocked. The refrigerator was running and the milk in it fresh. Inary started the coffeemaker, staring at the mugs on the wooden tree. Three. Aunt Inary's green one, the one with yellow daisies she'd always chosen as a child, and a mug she'd never seen before—white, crisscrossed with black lines. Who did it belong to? she wondered uneasily.

Stop it—you're safe here!

Taking a deep breath, she touched the daisy mug with caressing fingers, reminded of how Aunt Inary had always poured a cup of coffee for her when she had one herself, not taking stock in the theory that coffee was bad for children. She hadn't cried for her aunt when the lawyer's letter came—how could she cry for the narrow, crabbed woman who told her not to offer affection indiscriminately?

"I am not your mother," her aunt had said. "I am not anyone's mother, nor do I intend to be. I know your father would like to foist you onto me for good but I've told him I won't have it. And I won't have you attaching yourself to me, either. Pay attention, child.

No good comes from clinging to people who don't
want you.''

And so Inary had learned not to cling to her father,
either. She'd only been a nuisance to him, a child
someone must take care of, preferably not him. Her
mother had died when she was so young that Inary
had no memory of her. Between ten and fifteen, she'd
had a stepmother she'd liked, but then Harriet had
divorced her father and once again she'd had no one.
Perhaps the cold, selfish man she knew as her father
had loved the woman who'd been her mother—who
could tell? He certainly hadn't acted as though he'd
loved her stepmother.

His sister Inary, who she'd been named after, had
never wanted to be bothered with man or child. Aunt
Inary had never married; she'd lived alone, isolated in
her house on Lake Superior. She tolerated Inary during the times her father left her there, teaching her
about plants and the animals in the woods and about
her own peculiar view of the world. In her way, she'd
been as good as she could be to young Inary.

There'd always been a cat, always a Manx tabby
named Tansy. Inary was never sure just how many
Tansys there'd been, since they were identical in appearance and disposition, but she'd loved them all.

Gilgamesh interrupted her reverie with a complaint
and she realized she'd forgotten to fill his bowl with
water.

''You can always trust a cat to know what's going
on,'' her aunt had often said. ''I've lost more than one
because I didn't realize what she was trying to tell me
until it was too late to protect the cat. But *I've* sur-
vived because of the cats. Never be without one—it's
too dangerous.''

Aunt Inary was full of incomprehensible aphorisms—one of the reasons her father called his sister crazy. Of course she did end up in Sweetgrass State Hospital, where she'd died. Inary sighed. No doubt that's exactly where she'd end up. Not as a patient but as a nurse.

She needed to work, and Sweetgrass was the nearest place she could expect to earn decent money in the economically depressed Upper Peninsula. *If* they'd hire her; she hadn't had much experience with the mentally ill.

Gilgamesh eased past her to the back door where he stopped and looked around at her, obviously waiting for her to open it.

"You've already been out," she told him.

He flicked his tail and yowled.

Giving up, she unlocked the door and opened it, walked through the small storm shed where split logs were stacked against the wall, and opened the outer door. Gilgamesh shot through it. She stood in the doorway watching him, shivering in her thin California jacket.

A large woodpile stood to the left of the shed, an ax embedded in an upended log that was obviously used as a chopping block. She didn't recall Aunt Inary ever using an ax or even owning one. Where had this one come from? Still, an ax was nothing to be nervous about—or was it? Though she tried to tell herself she was overreacting, she knew she wouldn't feel secure until she and the cats were inside with all the doors locked.

She called to Gilgamesh but, as usual, he took his time. When at last he decided he was ready to return to the house, she shooed him in as quickly as she could, closed the shed door and shot the bolt, then entered the kitchen and locked that door, too.

"There," she muttered. "Everyone's locked out."

"Not quite. You've locked me in, not out," a voice from behind her said. A man's voice.

Inary froze. He's followed me! she thought in panic, her heart lurching in her chest. Followed me from California. She forced herself to turn, dreading what she'd see, and was stunned to find herself confronting a man she'd never seen before.

He was definitely a stranger, and yet a part of her seemed to know him, to reach out to him in greeting. He blinked and, for a split second, she had the impression that on some subtle level—one she didn't understand—he welcomed her in the same way.

A moment later his cold expression belied what she thought she'd felt. "I'm Ford Werlich," he said, raising his hands a little from his sides, palms uppermost in the age-old gesture showing he intended no harm. "You must be Inary Cameron. I'm sorry if I've frightened you. I should have knocked rather than used my key to come in the front door."

"Your key?" She had to force the words past her dry throat.

"Now that you're here, I won't need it." He reached into his pocket and dropped a door key on the table.

Still staring at him, Inary tried to gather her wits while she took inventory. Ford Werlich was dark-haired, a bit over medium height, sturdy, with a broad chest. His words sounded pleasant enough but his expression remained cold—no smile brought warmth to his closed, sharp-angled face. Noting his casual clothes, she decided he must be the caretaker the lawyer had hired.

"I saw your car," he went on, "so I came over to ask if you needed anything."

Came over? What was he talking about?

"Why don't you sit down?" he asked. "I see you've made coffee, and you look as though you could use a cup. I'll have one with you."

She bristled at his assumption that she'd want to have coffee with a stranger, but she didn't move or speak as he unhooked two mugs from the tree—the daisy one and the black-and-white mug—and set them on the table. He took a sugar bowl and matching creamer from one of the cupboards, opened the refrigerator and poured milk into the creamer. Resentment finally broke through her subsiding fear. This was her house—how dare he act as host?

"I've been getting the place ready for you," he said as he poured the coffee.

Inary pushed herself away from the door and advanced toward him, stopping when she reached the table. "I told no one I was coming," she said. "How could you know?"

"Your aunt told me you'd be here."

"Aunt Inary? But she's dead."

He waved an impatient hand. "We came to an agreement before she died. I was to keep this house in constant readiness for you, fires lit, stocked with food, beds made up and so on. In exchange, she deeded me some of her land to build on. I've since put a prefab log cabin on the property. We're neighbors."

Inary frowned. Neighbors? Aunt Inary had given him some of the land she'd sworn never to sell?

"Don't look so unhappy," he said. "I'm a good neighbor."

He still hadn't smiled. She noticed gray flecks in his dark hair, but he didn't look any older than his early thirties. He sounded frank, but his face remained cold and closed.

"I wasn't aware of any of this," she said at last. "The lawyer mentioned someone was looking after the place, but I didn't realize he meant what you've done."

"The lawyer wasn't involved in the arrangement other than making the agreement legal. This was between Miss Cameron and me." He pushed the filled daisy mug toward her.

"Exactly who are you?"

"I told you—Ford Werlich. I'm a psychiatrist at Sweetgrass. You do know your aunt was a patient there?"

A psychiatrist? Was his look asking her where she had been when her aunt needed her? Inary tightened her mouth. She was damned if she'd tell him she hadn't heard anything about it until after her aunt was dead and buried. Her answer was a curt nod.

He gestured for her to sit. When she didn't, he pulled one of the benches out and seated himself, spooning sugar into the steaming coffee in the black-and-white mug.

The rich aroma of the coffee teased Inary. With ill grace, she sat on the opposite bench, adding milk to her daisy mug.

When she glanced up, she thought she'd surprised a smile in his eyes but, if so, it faded immediately, never reaching his lips.

"Do you know what was wrong with my aunt?" she asked.

"The doctor in Norwich was convinced she had delusions and didn't believe it was safe for her to live alone, so he persuaded her nearest relative she belonged at Sweetgrass."

"Nearest relative" meant her father, who'd never called or written to tell her about Aunt Inary. Even after she'd died, it had been the lawyer who'd written her, not her father.

"Delusions," she said slowly. "That means she thought she was experiencing things that weren't really happening."

"Actually, I don't think there was anything wrong with your aunt's mind," he said.

"Then why was she kept at Sweetgrass?"

"I believe she thought of the place as a refuge. How well do you remember her?"

"Not too well," Inary admitted. "I was here off and on, sometimes during the school year, sometimes in the summer—it depended on my father's work. As an engineer he was often sent to foreign countries. The last time I saw my aunt was when I was fifteen." Inary took a sip of coffee. "She wasn't a person you got close to and yet she had a way of making me feel important. But I can't deny she was odd."

"Definitely odd," he agreed. "No question about it. But not psychotic and not senile, either. Miss Cameron's mind was as clear as mine, but she didn't want to come back to this house, she wanted to stay where she was, and so I helped her do as she wished. She never tried to fool me—she knew I wouldn't give her away."

Inary couldn't understand why anyone would want to remain in a state hospital. Her expression must have showed this, because Ford added, "She'd grown afraid of being alone in this house. I was trying to find a good nursing home for her when she died in her sleep."

Aunt Inary had never been afraid of anything, but maybe people grew more fearful as they aged. She'd died at eighty-two.

Though she'd made up her mind not to apologize for anything, Inary found herself saying, "My aunt and I had a—a disagreement the last time I visited here, when I was fifteen. She told both me and my father I couldn't come back, and I never did. Until now."

His lips twitched as though he might be going to smile, and she watched fascinated, wondering what she'd said to amuse him. The smile died before it was born, and Ford frowned.

"You're obviously wary of me," he said, "and I can't blame you. Strange as it may seem to you, your aunt trusted me from the moment we met. She told me she knew you were in danger and that you'd be needing a sanctuary."

Cradling the mug, he gazed at Inary, who was all but gaping at him in shock. "You have the same tawny eyes as she did. 'All the Cameron women do,' she told me. 'The gift is passed only to the females, along with the yellow cat's eyes.'"

Inary shook her head in confusion. Danger, sanctuary, yellow eyes, gifts—it was too much.

"I realize you're unaware of your gift," he said. "Your aunt wanted it kept that way for your own safety, so I won't offer to teach you. I've done what she asked me, all in all."

"You mean keeping this house in order?" Inary asked, grasping at something she could understand.

"Our agreement was that during my lifetime I'd watch over the house. Miss Cameron was positive you'd come, sooner or later. 'I won't live long,' she told me. 'I'm too old to prepare her a place of safety. I trust you to act in my stead.'"

Inary stared into her coffee mug as if the milky liquid would reveal the truth of this muddle. Her head whirled with fatigue.

"You're tired," he said. "We'll talk tomorrow. One last question—are you afraid to be alone here tonight?"

She blinked. "No."

"There's no phone—your aunt refused to have one put in."

"I remember. I'll see about getting a phone."

He rose from the bench. "If you'll come with me to the front door, I'll show you where I live."

"I didn't see another house when I drove in," she said, following him from the kitchen.

Standing in the open front door, cold air swirling around them, he pointed. "To the northwest, there, behind that clump of birch. I'll be home if you need me."

Inary nodded, unable to imagine asking for his help. Yet he seemed to mean well. "Thank you," she told him.

He laid a hand on her shoulder, the first time he'd touched her, and a jolt shot through her at the contact. He drew his hand away so fast she decided he'd felt it, too.

"You're sure you'll be all right?" he asked.

"I'll be fine," she managed to say, still wondering exactly what had happened when his hand rested so briefly on her shoulder. She'd felt his touch with every fiber of her being. It was different from man-woman chemistry; nothing remotely like it had ever happened to her before.

His brown eyes met hers, a dark, deep brown with amber wedges in the irises. There was still no trace of a smile on his lips. He nodded, turned and strode off toward the birches.

Gilgamesh tried to push past her, awakening her to the fact that she was standing with the door open, staring after Ford Werlich. She thwarted the cat's move and quickly closed the door, locking it and pushing the bolt across, as well.

She'd never met a man so somber. Why had her aunt trusted him? He'd kept his word, but it seemed to Inary he'd gotten the better of their bargain—her aunt's land. Mistrust budded inside her.

"I swore I'd never be like my father," she told Gilgamesh, "and here I am getting as suspicious as he always is. But in this case maybe I should be."

She climbed the stairs with the cat at her heels and found Enkidu had returned to the quilt on the fourposter. He slitted his eyes and yawned when they entered.

"I suppose you expect me to sleep here," she said to him. He closed his eyes, obviously not intending to move.

Though the bedroom had been her aunt's, Inary agreed with Enkidu's choice. She'd make it hers.

After fixing a temporary sandbox in the bathroom because she was too tired to let the cats out for a last run, Inary undressed and climbed into the bed, Enkidu on her left and Gilgamesh to her right, as usual.

A year ago, when she was living in the Sierra foothills, her apartment mate had brought Gilgamesh home as a pet. He'd been aloof even as a half-grown gray kitten, his white vest making him look absurdly formal. From the first, he'd preferred Inary and, when Joanne left to be married, Inary kept the cat.

One morning Gilgamesh had found Enkidu in the orange grove near the apartment, a pitiful ball of wet black fur, sick and shivering after a night rain. He'd supervised every step of the rescue process, licking the small cat's fur into shape after Inary brought him home and toweled him dry. From then on the pair were inseparable.

They'd saved Inary from the whisperer, and now she'd brought all three of them to safety. Their purring was the last thing she heard before she slipped into the dark vault of sleep....

She woke to whispering. "Rise," the beckoning voice insisted. "Rise and come to me."

"No," she quavered, but she found herself powerless to resist obeying. She floated from bedroom to living room, unable to stop despite her terror of the one who summoned her.

Helpless to do otherwise, she unlocked the front door and opened it. At that moment Gilgamesh twisted between her ankles, and she stepped on him. He wailed and she lost her balance, falling sideways as Enkidu slipped through the open door into an eerie, cloaking grayness.

Holding Gilgamesh, she stared apprehensively into the gray mist. Though her compulsion to obey the whisper had vanished, she felt certain danger lurked in the concealing tule fog. Enkidu refused to come when she called, and she feared for him but was afraid to leave the security of her doorway.

Suddenly Gilgamesh, his fur standing on end, leaped from her arms and vanished into the fog. Barefoot and in her nightgown, she ran after him, desperately calling both cats. A heart-rending yowl answered her. Her skin prickled with terror as she groped her way toward the frantic caterwauling.

Her way was blocked by tree branches and the golden globes of oranges, unseen until she blundered into them. At last a flash of white caught her eye. Through the mist she saw Gilgamesh, his back hunched, all his hair raised, mouth drawn back so his teeth showed. He spat at her when she reached for him.

Then she saw the huddled black body behind him and the blood on the shiny steel jaws of the trap....

CHAPTER TWO

Inary woke to darkness, shivering with leftover fear
from the dream that hadn't been so much a dream as
a ghastly reliving of what had happened to poor
Enkidu. She switched on the lamp beside the bed,
rousing the cats who blinked sleepily at her. It was 2:00
a.m.

All three of them were safe, she assured herself,
unable to be rid of the disturbing shards of dream and
memory. Only too well she remembered crouching
beside Enkidu in grief and horror, certain he was dead.
He lay without moving, his right front paw nearly
severed, blood staining the trap and dark on the
ground beside him. She touched him gently and felt his
chest rise and fall under her hand. He was alive!

Then a figure had loomed dark in the thinning early
morning fog and she tensed until she recognized the
man as Manuel Gomez, the caretaker of the orange
grove. He had no idea who'd set the trap and he was
angry that it should be in the grove. He used his knife
to cut away the shreds of tissue holding Enkidu's leg
in the trap, then brought Gilgamesh back to her
apartment while she carried the still-bleeding Enkidu.

After Manuel left, saying he was going to get rid of
"that damned trap," she dressed hurriedly and drove
Enkidu to the vet.

Later, she'd asked Manuel what he'd done with the trap and he'd told her it was gone when he returned to the grove, that both trap and Enkidu's severed paw had vanished. He hadn't liked it at all and neither had she.

Early the following morning, Inary had found Gilgamesh sitting by the front door, growling, his hair bristling. She could see no one through the spy lens. When she finally gathered enough courage to unlock and open the door, a cat's paw, Enkidu's paw, stiff with dried blood, swung on the outside knob, attached by a thin braid of blond hair. Her hair. Then she'd known who'd set the trap. Then she'd known she had to flee.

"So here we are," she said to the cats, finding the sound of her own voice startling in the quiet night. "Safe and sound on the shores of Gitche Gumee." God, how she hoped it was true!

Gilgamesh rose, stretched and settled down again, a reassuring sight since it meant he sensed no danger. Though Inary couldn't bring herself to shut off the lamp, she finally fell asleep again.

The next she knew it was daylight and Enkidu was sitting on her stomach staring at her with reproachful yellow eyes. Gilgamesh yowled impatiently from somewhere downstairs. "Okay, so you're hungry," she muttered.

But when she pulled on a robe and went down into the kitchen, both cats were sitting by the back door, clearly wanting out. Telling herself nothing would harm them in these woods, she opened both the back and the shed doors and watched Gilgamesh dash into the trees with Enkidu following awkwardly behind.

In the kitchen, the stove was cold, the fire out. If she wanted anything hot for breakfast she'd have to use the hot plate, so she decided to stick to toast and coffee. Sooner or later, she'd have to learn how to use the wood range.

Today was Sunday and she could afford to be lazy, but she had to keep in mind that what was left of her money wouldn't last long. Tomorrow she'd arrange for a phone and apply for a job at Sweetgrass.

Once Inary got dressed and fed herself and the cats, she stepped into the sunny and crisp March morning with the cats at her heels. At the rear of the house, the lake side, a white-pine grove rose beyond the still-leafless maples that guarded the house. The shade of the tall virgin trees discouraged undergrowth, so there was nothing beneath them except a thick carpet of brown needles.

As she started through the pines, a blue jay screeched a warning of her approach and she searched overhead, finding the bright blue and white bird with his smart black trim perched on a high branch. Michigan jays were a true bright blue, not the gray-blue of the scrub jays in California. Her feet grew cold in her sandals but she continued along a remembered, scarcely visible path through the trees until she stood on the white-sand beach with Lake Superior quiescent before her. The water quivered like quicksilver in the pale sunlight, the waves easing lazily onto the sand.

Taking a deep breath, Inary told herself: I'm home.

A nasty little north wind blew, not ruffling the lake but sneaking under her light jacket to chill her so she had to keep moving to stay warm. Walking west along the beach, she didn't admit to herself she was looking for Ford until she saw him ahead of her and her heart lurched, annoying her.

As though sensing her behind him, he stopped and turned. "I've been waiting for you," he said.

She raised her eyebrows, immediately wary.

"I forgot to mention the fires," he said. "I'm willing to bet you let the kitchen stove go out."

She nodded. "The fireplace, too. But there's central heating—the house is warm enough."

"The fireplace has heat vents. If you keep it going you'll use less oil. There's plenty of free wood lying around."

Inary frowned at being told what to do. Still, she had no doubt oil *was* expensive and she did have to watch her money.

"I'm not much of a fire-starter," she admitted.

"I'll teach you. By May it'll be time to remove the storm windows and replace them with the screens. If you like, I'll show you how."

"That's kind of you." She was reluctant to depend on him, but she'd never put screens on windows in her life. Or kindled a wood stove.

"I'll be around to help you learn the tricks of dealing with your old house," he said, making her almost believe he'd read her mind. "As well as anything else you might need to learn."

Before she could react to the undercurrent running through his last few words, he strode ahead, turning into the trees toward her house. She followed, irritated without being certain why. She might need to learn how to manage wood ranges and old storm windows, but there was certainly nothing else she wanted him to teach her!

When she caught up, he'd found Enkidu and was cuddling the cat in his arms. The cat, usually nervous in the presence of strangers, appeared quite content in Ford's embrace.

"I noticed yesterday that he was missing a paw," Ford said. "What happened?"

She fought down the urge to snatch the cat from him and retreat to the house, shutting him out. "He lost the paw in a trap," she said as calmly as she could. "In California."

The horror of that moment in the orange grove, so vividly relived in last night's dream, came back to her and she bit her lip, her hands clenching into fists.

Ford focused on her, his brown gaze as compelling and arrogant as Gilgamesh's imperious green stare. "So your aunt was right." His voice was soft and, unless she was mistaken, regretful.

"Right about what?"

"When she told me you were in danger."

Inary fumbled for a response, not wanting to lie outright and at the same time unwilling to trust this cold-eyed stranger with anything approximating the truth. "I can't understand why Aunt Inary would believe I was in danger," she said finally.

Gilgamesh darted from between two trees onto the path in front of them and, instead of pursuing the subject, Ford asked, "Any more cats?"

Welcoming the shift, she said, "No. He's Gilgamesh. You're holding Enkidu. They stayed on the sidelines sizing you up yesterday. Apparently you've passed muster."

"With all three of you?"

"With the cats."

Ford stroked Enkidu's long black fur. "So, hairy one," he said to the cat, "you're a fighter like your namesake. But be careful—he lost in the end."

Inary warmed to him. He liked cats and he knew mythology—he couldn't be all bad. She might even offer him a cup of coffee after he showed her how to keep the fire burning in the wood range.

"Your aunt's keys are in the top desk drawer in her den," Ford said as they came into the kitchen. "The one to the room in the attic seems to be missing, though. I cleaned the rest of the attic at her request but I've no idea what's inside that room because the door's locked. She didn't give me a key to it, and I haven't found one in the house."

Inary looked at him blankly. "The attic's all open space. There's never been a separate room up there."

Ford frowned. "Maybe Miss Cameron had one built since you were here last, because there's definitely a room now."

"But I was in the attic yesterday and I didn't see one."

He grasped her hand and once again she felt the shock of the contact jolt through her. Pulling her with him, he propelled her up the two flights of stairs, not letting her go until they stood under the tower skylight.

"There," he said, pointing. "See the door?"

She shook her head. "I see a wall." Turning to stare at him, she wondered in rising alarm why he was trying to make her see a nonexistent door, why he talked about a locked room that wasn't here. Was he crazy?

"Look at Gilgamesh," he advised.

The big gray cat had followed them to the attic and now crouched, growling, in front of the wall in question. The cat retreated, backing slowly away from the wall, his fur bristling. She could all but feel the cat's fear. But of what? His reaction made her arms prickle with gooseflesh.

When he reached the steps, Gilgamesh turned and fled down them. Inary swallowed, disturbed by the cat's obvious fright. Ford's strong fingers closed around hers again and he led her across to the wall.

"Close your eyes," he said, his voice as gentle as when he'd spoken to Enkidu.

"Why?" she demanded, intent on not revealing how nervous he and the cat had made her.

"Humor me."

Shrugging, she obeyed. Still holding her hand, he raised it until she touched the wall. Only it wasn't wood she felt under her fingers but the cool roundness of a metal doorknob. Shocked, she opened her eyes, only to find Ford's other hand blocking her vision.

"I'll uncover your eyes very soon, Inary," he said, his voice low and measured. "When I do, you'll not only see the knob you hold but the door it's attached to. There's a room behind the door. When I remove my hand you'll see the door." As his hand fell away, he released his grip on her other hand and stepped back.

She stared unbelievingly at the door, her fingers clenching as they turned the knob. The door remained closed. Locked, as he'd said.

Inary whirled to face him. "Why couldn't I see this until now?" she cried, fear clutching at her.

Did her failure to know the room existed somehow tie in with her fugue states? She hoped not. The medicine her California doctor had prescribed had re-

duced the incidence of what she still thought of by her
stepmother's name for them—her spells. She hadn't
had a spell for over six months, not even one of those
weird feelings that sometimes came over her. Was not
seeing things that were actually there a new symp-
tom?

"What's wrong with me?" she whispered more to
herself than to Ford.

"Nothing's wrong," he said. "My guess is your
aunt didn't want you to know the room was here so
she made a post-hypnotic suggestion to you as a child
telling you that you wouldn't be able to see a door in
the attic. She probably reinforced the suggestion every
time you came to stay with her."

"Are you saying Aunt Inary hypnotized me? That's
impossible!"

"Is it? Think back. You can remember if you
choose to."

Inary started to shake her head in annoyance—he
couldn't be right—when suddenly candle flames
seemed to flicker before her eyes and she felt herself
sliding away, spiraling into another place and time.

*She was standing before an open door, looking at
her aunt who was sitting Indian-fashion on a dark red
rug with a book open on her lap.*

*Her aunt saw her, rose and led her inside, holding
her so she faced the candle. "Watch the candle, the
fire, the flame." Aunt Inary spoke in a singsong.
"Watch the flickering flame dance closer. Watch the
fire dance. Watch. Watch and listen.*

"Time goes in

"Time goes out

"I stand within

"You stand without..."

Inary heard someone call her name from a long way off, repeating it over and over until she could no longer focus on the candles or her aunt's chanting. She felt arms around her, holding her; they were no longer her aunt's arms but a man's. She knew it couldn't be her father. She tried to think who it might be, to look, but fire burned between them and she couldn't see past the bright flame.

Warm lips covered hers, bringing the brilliant shimmer of the fire inside her. His close embrace promised delights she'd never known, and she realized she was no longer a child, she was a woman. Longing for what he alone could give her, she responded to the seeking demand of the kiss, offering herself without restraint.

Without warning, the warmth and closeness vanished. She felt the eternal chill of being alone and murmured a protest, reaching, wanting.

"It does no good to cling, Inary...." The echo of her aunt's voice warned her.

The spell ended abruptly, bringing her back to the here and now. Inary opened her eyes to find herself supine on the floor with Ford Werlich kneeling beside her but not touching her. "You're back," he said softly. The sharp planes of his face hadn't changed but the coldness was gone.

Had he really kissed her? Her mind roiled in chaos, reality broken into jigsaw puzzle pieces she couldn't fit together properly. How she hated these spells! Involuntarily, she raised her hands to her lips as though to feel if the kiss still lingered there.

Ford's mouth twitched in response. "You do remember, then."

He *had* kissed her.

"I couldn't rouse you from the trance you fell into when you recalled what happened between you and your aunt years ago," he said. "So I tried a bit of shock therapy."

Shock therapy. Is that what he called it? And she'd responded. Resentment trickled through her, as much from the fact that he now knew she had these spells as from his words. She turned away from him, finding herself looking at the door to the locked room. Instantly the pieces fit together, and she sat up.

"That door was open," she said, remembering. "I started to go in and my aunt did something to make me forget—hypnotized me, I suppose. I was quite young, I think. Maybe my first summer here. I'd come up to the attic to look for Tansy—" She paused. "What happened to Tansy—my aunt's cat?"

"Miss Cameron told me her two-year-old cat disappeared shortly before she was committed to Sweetgrass. I've searched the woods for the cat but found no sign of her." He stood and helped Inary to her feet. "Are you all right now?"

"I feel confused," she admitted, firmly resisting a vagrant impulse to lean against him. "The door, remembering how my aunt chanted—it was as though I could hear her all over again."

"You repeated her words during your trance."

Inary shifted her shoulders uneasily. "Those words about time going in and out, it's as if there's power hidden in them."

"There is."

She shook her head. "I don't want to think so. I hate having what you call trances. I don't like the rug of rationality pulled out from under my feet. Nothing should be inexplicable—that's what my science courses taught me. Cause and effect. Reasons. Answers. But ever since the man in the quarry, the world's grown more and more frightening, and I can't find answers.''

''What man in the quarry?'' Ford asked.

She hadn't meant to mention the red-haired man; it was best to keep the terrifying events of the past from invading her mind. ''No,'' she said, meaning she refused to discuss it. He seemed to understand for he didn't press her.

Inary noticed that both cats had come into the attic, ranging themselves between her and the locked door with their hair bristling. ''What do they sense?'' she asked.

''Wrongness. I sense it, too. No wonder your aunt blocked its very existence from your mind. I hope the key stays lost—that room's best kept locked forever. Let's get out of here.''

More than ready to go, she didn't argue.

Learning the intricacies of the wood range cleared her mind, banishing the residue of uneasiness. When Ford actually smiled in approval at the way she handled the dampers, she wanted to cheer.

''You should smile more often,'' she told him when they sat down with their mugs of coffee.

''I haven't found much to smile about lately.''

''I suppose working at Sweetgrass might be depressing. Whether it is or not, I'm going to apply for work as a nurse there.''

The cold, watchful look settled over his face again. ''Why not try one of the community hospitals in the towns around here?''

"I'm sure the state offers better pay and benefits. I don't mind working, but I do like to be paid a decent wage."

Unexpectedly, he smiled. "Nurses never get paid as much as they're worth. You ought to have discovered that by now."

She rolled her eyes. "Tell me."

"Pay aside, I'm not certain working at Sweetgrass would suit you," he said.

A small cloud of suspicion shadowed the rapport building between them. Was there some reason he didn't want her applying for a job at the same place where he worked? Did he have something to hide? Something to do with her aunt?

"I'm adaptable," she said lightly.

"Are you?" The somber tone was back in his voice. He took a final swallow of coffee and rose, looking down at her. "Promise me something."

Finding his standing over her somewhat intimidating, she got to her feet. "I don't make blind promises."

"If you should run across the key to that attic room, I want you to let me know. And for God's sake, don't ever try to go into the room without me."

"Since you couldn't find the key, I doubt that I will," she said, avoiding a yes-or-no answer, though she certainly had no intention of ever exploring that room alone. In fact, she wished she still didn't know it was there. "I certainly don't expect to waste my time searching."

"I have the feeling your aunt's hidden the key and that she told you where, then ordered you to forget you knew the hiding place until something triggered your memory. That may happen, Inary. Please let me know if you find the key."

He'd said please, remarkable for Ford. "If you insist," she conceded.

When he left by way of the front door, she stood watching him until he was hidden by the trees. When she became aware she was brushing her forefinger over her lips, she grimaced and slammed the door.

He told you it was nothing but shock therapy, you romantic idiot, she admonished herself.

Ford skirted the tangle of bare-branched birches, then strode through the pines to his log cabin. He flung open the door and kicked it shut behind him. He'd thought he knew enough about Inary Cameron to cope with her when and if she arrived. So much for smugness.

He might be a board-certified psychiatrist as well an expert in more esoteric knowledge but he'd neglected to remember that he was a man and she was a woman. Neither psychiatry nor witchcraft had any explanation—or remedy—for the volatile chemistry between the sexes, the inexplicable attraction that made fools of even the strongest and most rational of humans.

After listening to her aunt, he'd prepared himself to be drawn to the shimmer of Inary's power, one adept recognizing the potential of another. That was a given, whether the possessor was a man or a woman and, by itself, not at all sexual.

Seeing her for the first time had been a pleasant surprise. Miss Cameron had shown him a picture of her niece at thirteen, a photo that had vaguely hinted at the promise of beauty to come. And come it certainly had. He was no different than most men; he liked good-looking women. Her hair was the color of fine, pale sherry, her eyes as golden as topaz. She had to be about three inches shorter than his five-ten, slender but well curved.

Pretty as she was, he hadn't been overwhelmed, even though he'd also been aware, as she obviously was not, of her aura of power. Then he'd made the mistake of resting his hand on her shoulder. He'd spent most of the night trying to convince himself he'd only imagined the electrifying surge that sizzled through him. A damn sight more than sexual attraction was involved.

He'd already learned that touching her was risky, but he'd taken her hand to lead her into the attic and then, with all the more reliable and far safer methods he might have used to bring her out of that unexpected trance, he'd kissed her instead.

Shock therapy, he'd called it, but who'd gotten the greater shock?

He'd meant to be very careful with her, to bring her gradually to the realization of her potential. To reach that goal he had to gain her trust. He'd sure as hell blown that expectation to shreds.

Get a grip on yourself, Werlich, he ordered. You know what happened the last time you lost your cool. One disaster a lifetime is more than enough.

If Inary went to work at Sweetgrass—and he could hardly stop her—sooner or later she'd hear the rumors about him. What then? Even if he overcame that handicap, there was still the possible menace of the locked room. Miss Cameron had never revealed its secret; she'd refused to discuss it at all, other than once saying, "I'm far enough away from what's inside that room here at Sweetgrass. I'm safe."

He took a deep breath and let it out slowly, knowing he was too tense to initiate meditation—maybe a little Dixieland would help him relax.

Shuffling through his CDs, he wondered about the man in the quarry. Someone who coveted what Inary didn't yet know she possessed, he had no doubt. He hoped that like many adepts, the man was bound to one certain place of power, the quarry she'd mentioned, because this would keep him in California, unable to follow Inary.

But even if the man in the quarry remained where he was, that didn't mean others with dark powers wouldn't sense her presence and lust for what she could give them, others much closer than California.

Ford wanted to help Inary—he meant to help her despite his own newfound need to possess her—but he didn't expect it to be easy. The situation here was already explosive enough without adding any more unknown factors. Or actors.

He flicked on the stereo and the high wail of a clarinet filled the room, Pete Fountain climbing into "A Taste Of Honey." Ford's smile was wry. Honey, yes, and a lot more besides. Inary had responded to his kiss for a beat or two, but chances were she hadn't realized what she was doing. Even if she had been fully aware and wanted everything he'd wanted, he couldn't have gone on making love to her. It wouldn't have been fair.

First she had to discover what she was. After that she could decide which path to take. Until then, her only protection was Ford Werlich, but now that he'd met her, he couldn't be sure he might not turn out to be her greatest peril.

CHAPTER THREE

On Tuesday, after Inary's phone was installed, she called Sweetgrass State Hospital and was told they had openings for registered nurses. She'd never actually been to Sweetgrass since the town itself, as well as the nearby hospital, were both off the state highway. The closest she'd come to either was driving past with her father when she was a child and he was bringing her to stay with her aunt.

Sweetgrass was, she discovered the next day, thirty miles from Norwich, the village closest to her house on the lake. *Her* house. She felt a thrill every time she remembered that the old place actually belonged to her. She'd found a sanctuary when she needed one most. Or, rather, her aunt had willed her the sanctuary.

As she drove into the hospital entrance she noticed the buildings were what she'd always thought of as institutional brick. Though they had no pretensions to gracefulness or beauty, their uncompromisingly square outlines were muted by the huge pines and spruces that had grown through the years and now shut the hospital away from the community.

Personnel confirmed that they needed registered nurses—and she was hired because her California RN license was valid in Michigan, or would be after the hospital checked with Sacramento. After filling out innumerable forms in triplicate, and following an interview with the director of nurses, she was introduced to the assistant director, Mrs. Havighurst, a tall, emaciated woman in a white uniform who wore a conical white cap atop clipped white hair.

"Since you'll be working in the new building, I'll tour you through it while you're here," Mrs. Havighurst told her as they left the administration building. "Ordinarily we don't place our new nurses on a unit until they've completed our ten-day orientation but, unfortunately, at the moment we're critically short of RNs, especially on the evening shift."

"I understand," Inary said.

"Naturally, we'll orient you as soon as possible. Over there—" the assistant director pointed "—is the infants' and children's unit, the C building, where you'll be."

Inary gazed across brown lawns and through the leafless branches of tall maples at a building whose bricks didn't quite match the others. Recently planted spruce trees were yet too young to soften the building's outlines.

"You'll be assigned to the functionally disabled unit, C2," Mrs. Havighurst went on.

Having worked in pediatric wards, Inary felt fairly secure. Children were children, after all, whatever their abilities. Or disabilities.

Some minutes later, as they passed through C1, a unit of bed patients, and she was confronted by the misshapen heads of hydrocephalics and the grotesquely twisted bodies of spastics, she changed her mind. This would take some getting used to.

After leaving C1, Mrs. Havighurst paused before a closed door, selected a key from her metal ring and inserted it into the lock. "C2," she announced. "Where you'll be working."

"A locked unit?" Inary asked.

"It's necessary to prevent these children from wandering away and getting lost. Most are ambulatory and some are hyperactive."

When the door closed behind them, locking automatically, Inary quickly discovered what the assistant director meant. They were overwhelmed by a swarm of children of all sizes and all stages of cleanliness. Hands touched Inary, clutching at her. She drew back, green mucus smeared on her hand from a runny nose. She was ashamed of her instinctive withdrawal, but the children's desperate seeking for attention and affection appalled her.

I've always liked children, she reminded herself. When I get used to them I'll feel differently.

A big woman in a blue uniform swept down the hall, scattering the children. As they dispersed, Inary noticed a girl of about five crouched in a corner, her dark hair pulled over her face. Bright eyes stared through the strands of hair and, when Inary's gaze met the child's, she had the strangest feeling that the little girl was reaching out to her in some undefinable way. Before she had a chance to do or say anything, Mrs. Havighurst introduced her to the large woman.

"This is Ms. Beech. She's been a nurse assistant with us here for years. You'll find her pleasant to work with, I'm sure." Turning to Ms. Beech, the assistant director said, "Ms. Cameron will be starting as charge nurse on evenings beginning Friday."

Inary and Ms. Beech exchanged measuring glances and nodded tentatively but had no chance to talk to each other before the assistant director began shepherding Inary toward the door. As she left the unit, Inary looked back. The little girl was no longer in the corner or anywhere in sight.

After leaving the hospital, Inary did her grocery shopping in Sweetgrass. As she drove home, she puzzled over the unusual experience with the withdrawn little girl, dwelling on that rather than giving in to worry about starting her new job. Beginnings were always a bit difficult for her, but she had confidence in her ability to cope. No doubt she'd adjust quickly. Or so she hoped.

Back at the house, she changed into jeans and a heavy sweatshirt before donning her jacket and taking the path to the lake, Gilgamesh running ahead and Enkidu trailing her. When she reached the water's edge, she paused, facing into the brisk, chill wind as she watched the continuous roll of the waves—white-capped today.

Gradually her gaze was drawn to the west where a spit of land thrust a long finger into the lake. This point marked the western boundary of her aunt's—no, of *her* land. A wide creek separated the point from the rest of her property. While the point was an uncomfortable reminder of why she'd been exiled from here for so many years, at the same time, inexplicably, she was drawn to it.

"Agate Point." Ford's voice came from behind her. Though he'd startled her, she deliberately didn't turn. "I know the name," she said.

"I've found some unusual and beautiful agates on the beach there," he said, coming up to stand beside her.

Did he think she wasn't aware the pebble-strewn beach of the point was littered with agates? She certainly was overly aware of him and the fact that the two of them were alone on an isolated beach. "I didn't expect to see you on a working day," she said as casually as she could.

"I'm taking some of the comp time due me for being on call at the hospital."

"I'm starting at Sweetgrass on Friday," she said.

After a moment's silence he asked, "Where?"

"The functionally disabled children's unit."

"C2. Did you happen to meet Mouse yet?"

About to say no, she paused, for some reason recalling the child in the corner. "A little girl who peers at you through her hair?" she asked.

"You've met her, then."

"Not exactly. But—" She broke off, uncertain she wanted to tell him any more.

"So she got to you already. Interesting."

Inary stared at him. "What do you mean?"

He shrugged. "We'll discuss it after you've been working on C2 for a while." He nodded toward the point. "Care to take a walk?"

She held back her instinctive *No!*, saying, "I don't imagine the old railroad bridge over the creek is still passable. Years ago, when I visited here, many of the ties were almost rotted through and crossing them was a gamble even then."

"Some of them have fallen into the creek since you were last here. I've thrown planks across the worst of the gaps but I admit it's still risky."

Relieved he'd offered a reason to refuse, she said, "With this cold March wind blowing, I don't think I care to chance being dunked in icy creek water."

"We'll head in the other direction, then," he said, reaching down to scoop up Enkidu, who was sitting on his shoe. He started walking east without waiting for her to agree or refuse.

"I thought psychiatrists were supposed to stay attuned to people," she fumed when she caught up with him. "Didn't it occur to you I might not want to take a stroll along the beach with you?"

He glanced at her. "We're neighbors, with no one else living anywhere near us. Life is less complicated if neighbors get along with one another and even easier if they become friends. Walking is one way to become better acquainted. As a reasonable human being, why would you refuse to walk with me?"

His logic annoyed her. The sight of Enkidu, curled contentedly in Ford's arms, irked her even more. "I suppose he's even purring," she muttered.

"As a matter of fact, he is. Enkidu and I feel an affinity for each another, just as you and Gilgamesh share a closeness. I realize you're upset with me over what happened in the attic, but what did you expect? That I wouldn't try to rectify things once I realized you'd been hypnotized into forgetting the room was there? Letting it go would have been far too dangerous."

"Dangerous?" Her voice rose. "Why do you keep harping about danger?"

He smiled one-sidedly. "*Harping*. I like that word. Your aunt used it, too. Puts me in mind of old-world itinerant harpers singing of ancient days and daring deeds."

What an infuriating conversation, Inary thought. Why couldn't he give a straightforward answer to a simple question? But if he thought to distract her, he was wrong.

"Danger," she repeated firmly. "What danger?"

His smile faded, wariness replacing it. "Danger waits inside the locked room, as I told you. At least you're aware now that the room exists. And, when you find the hidden key, I hope you have enough sense to think twice before using it."

"You don't make sense. If I wasn't aware of the room, how would I have known which lock the key fit, supposing I'd found it?"

"I suspect finding the key would have triggered your memory of the room and voided your aunt's post-hypnotic suggestion of forgetfulness. I didn't dare take the chance you might walk blindfolded into danger."

Inary scowled. "I still don't understand how that locked room can be dangerous. What's in there?"

"If I knew, I'd tell you. You don't have to take my word about the danger—you saw the reaction of the cats, didn't you? Trust in them, if you don't trust me."

She didn't trust him. As for the cats—Inary sighed. She couldn't deny they'd saved her from very definite peril in California. In any case, since she wasn't likely to find the key if Ford had searched for it in vain, she might as well stop worrying about the attic room.

The truth was that Ford made her uneasy, putting her on the defensive. Though he wasn't so close that they touched as they ambled along near the water's edge, she had the impression she'd be able to feel his nearness even if she were, in fact, blindfolded. No man she'd ever met had affected her in quite this way—he seemed to give off a magnetic energy that made every nerve in her body vibrate with awareness.

She found it frightening.

Enkidu's purr vibrated through Ford, attuning him to the cat. Cradling the animal soothed him, blunting his need to touch Inary. And touching her, as he'd discovered, was not a good idea. If he was to be of any help to her, and God knows she needed help, he must remain as clinically detached as if she were one of his patients. From time to time he'd found himself attracted to a female patient but it had always been easy for him to conquer the feeling before it interfered with the doctor-patient relationship.

Unfortunately, what was between him and Inary was not simply sexual attraction, though that added to the problem. While she didn't need his clinical ability, she stood in desperate need of enlightenment in other spheres. If he couldn't maintain some degree of detachment, he'd be powerless to help her survive.

Since it was already obvious she meant to resist the truth, he faced the monumental task of fighting against his own urges while he struggled to first convince her there was a hidden path and then try to teach her how to best follow that path.

He took a deep breath and gazed at the lake, roughened by the still-wintry March wind. Running from his past, he'd chosen to escape to this harsh wilderness. Miss Cameron had viewed it differently.

"I've no doubt in my mind you were directed here, Doctor," she'd insisted. "No doubt at all. You were sent here to save Inary and you've come just in time to allow me to die in peace."

He hadn't argued with her, keeping his own doubts to himself, though he fully intended to keep his part of the bargain. But, in his heart of hearts, he hadn't really expected Miss Cameron's niece to ever come to live in the house he kept prepared for her.

Conscious they'd been walking in silence for some time, he said, "What shift are you working at the hospital?"

"Evenings," she said. "So it's clearly impossible for us to car-pool since I imagine you generally work days."

He thought she sounded relieved. "True, except when I'm on call." He glanced at his watch. "Since it appears I won't be seeing much of you after tomorrow, how about having coffee with me now. My treat."

"Well, I—"

"You haven't seen my house. And the cats may as well get used to my place."

She raised her eyebrows. "The cats?"

"Surely you don't intend to keep them inside all the time."

"No, not all the time. But I thought they'd be better off inside while I was working. I don't like them out at night."

He shrugged. She wasn't yet ready to have him try to explain why the cats should remain outside to protect the house while she was gone. "I imagine there'll be times they'll want to visit me," he said. "Enkidu and I are already buddies. And I think Gilgamesh has accepted me."

She nodded.

"So—coffee?"

Inary smiled. "I guess I'm not being very neighborly. Yes, thank you, I'd be delighted to join you for coffee."

Ford enjoyed his house. It might be prefab but the rooms were a decent size and he liked the rustic look of the log exterior. He'd had his few good pieces of furniture trucked up from the Lower Peninsula where they'd been in storage and he'd filled in with new and old pieces bought locally. Once he'd ushered Inary inside, he found himself waiting for her reaction, as though it really mattered to him.

"It's charming," she said, looking around. "When you said prefab I thought it would be like a mobile home, but I was wrong."

Gilgamesh, who'd followed them in, sauntered over to the hearth, smelled carefully around and then curled up on the rag rug in front of the dying fire. When Ford set Enkidu down on the floor, the long hair joined Gilgamesh.

"The cats are certainly making themselves at home." Inary's tone held surprise. "They're usually wary of strange places. And strange people."

"Then it's lucky I'm not a strange person."

Her level gaze suggested she wasn't entirely convinced.

He gestured toward the chairs cozily drawn up to the hearth. "We'll have coffee there. Sit down and I'll bring it."

He liked the way she didn't insist on giving him a hand, as though she knew if he wanted help, he'd ask. It was entirely possible, given the strong connection between them, that at some subconscious level she did know without realizing it.

When he returned from the kitchen and set the serving tray between them on a pull-up table, he found Inary sitting on one of the chairs, gazing into the glowing embers.

"They're like red eyes staring back at me," she said, and she shivered.

Since his house was warm, especially in front of the hearth, he knew she wasn't cold. "Red eyes," he echoed tentatively, much as he did when he wanted a patient to tell him more. It was often effective.

She glanced at him and shook her head. "Don't try any of your shrink techniques on me, Doctor. It's merely a silly fancy."

He let her explanation lie, busying himself with pouring the coffee and offering her the creamer. Then he sat back in his chair with his cup, looked at the coals rather than at her and waited a calculated few minutes before speaking. "Coming from California, I imagine you're into holistic medicine."

"Somewhat," she said. "I've found the laying on of hands seems to work quite well for me."

He wasn't surprised but he didn't say so. "What's your opinion of other new-age theories?" he asked.

"Oh, I don't know. It's difficult for me to believe in most of it."

"If you had to choose one facet to believe in, what would it be?" He watched her from the corner of his eye.

Inary bit her lip, staring into her coffee cup. "Maybe past lives," she said after a moment. "I can't really accept the idea, but I must admit it would explain a few things."

"Such as?"

She glanced at him. "You."

He raised an indolent eyebrow, careful to seem no more than casually interested.

"It's just that—" she began, then paused. He waited. "It may be a foolish notion," she finally went on, "but I have a strange feeling that you and I might have been—well, friends—once before. Somewhere."

If they'd known each other in a past life they sure as hell would have been a lot more than friends. "Don't you mean some*when?*" he corrected, giving her a one-sided smile.

"I suppose I must. And, really, I don't actually believe all this. Of course we'd never met before I arrived on Sunday—anywhere or anywhen—but I keep having this weird sensation that you're not a stranger."

Concealing his elation that she, too, felt their bonding, he said, "I'd like us to be friends."

Could she be friends with this cold-eyed man she didn't exactly trust? Inary asked herself. She wasn't yet sure. He'd warmed up considerably since their first meeting—hadn't he forgotten himself enough to smile at her three times? But his eyes remained cool and watchful.

She hadn't been able to shake her odd feeling that something invisible connected them in a way she didn't at all understand. Or even like. Still, it was there.

She had to admit the cats trusted Ford, so he couldn't be evil, like that red-haired man from the quarry. Their acceptance of him made her less nervous about him living so close to her, but she was reluctant to give her complete trust to anyone. Especially this man who'd somehow gotten her aunt to deed him enough land to build on. That wasn't like Aunt Inary, not at all.

She'd withhold judgment.

"You don't think we can be friends?"

Ford's question reminded her she hadn't replied. "I'm willing to try," she said cautiously. "If you promise not to spring any more dubious surprises like that locked attic door."

He shook his head. "Life being what it is, there's no guarantee against surprises, dubious or worse. Especially since Walpurgis Night is only a little over a month away."

Inary gaped at him. "What on earth is Walpurgis Night?"

"Technically, it's the night of April 30, the evening before May 1, that being the feast day of St. Walburgha. But the celebration is far older than the good saint. The Catholic church established Walburgha's feast day to mask or take the place of an ancient pagan celebration to welcome the return of spring."

"But what does all this have to do with me?"

"Nothing, I hope."

"Then why mention Walpurgis Night?"

"Because your aunt feared it. Even I—" He broke off, shrugging. "I shouldn't have brought it up so soon." He raised his coffee cup. "Shall we drink to our developing friendship?"

Inary hesitated but finally lifted her cup. Ford leaned forward to touch his cup to hers, then finished off his coffee, watching her until she took a sip of hers.

What had he meant by *so soon?* And why bring up the subject of the pagan rites of spring?

"You don't believe in such things do you?" she blurted. "Pagan rites and the like, I mean."

"If you mean do I celebrate Walpurgis Night, no, I do not. Just the opposite—I'm relieved each year when dawn comes on May 1. If you mean does anyone, anywhere still celebrate that dark and sinister eve—yes, they do. Unfortunately."

Inary tried to assimilate this. "What's dark and sinister about the night before a saint's feast day?" she wanted to know.

"Dark forces are stronger on Walpurgis Night, giving evil an edge over good."

As far as she could tell, Ford seemed perfectly sincere. He spoke calmly, he wasn't hiding a smirk and those dark eyes retained their wariness. And yet he couldn't possibly be serious. A psychiatrist believing in evil?

"I don't understand you at all," she snapped. "Why do you talk of dark forces and evil? I agree people sometimes commit atrocious crimes, but not because they're evil. People aren't evil, just maladjusted or crazy."

"Evil exists," Ford said evenly. "Evil is powerful and can possess people. Fortunately, good is also powerful, because we do need it to combat evil."

"You sound like an old-time preacher sermonizing about sinners and heaven and hell," she scoffed, hoping to ease her increasing anxiety by being flippant.

"Sinners are not my province and I have absolutely no knowledge of heaven or hell. But I do know about good and evil." To her surprise he suddenly grinned, even his eyes warming. Pointing at her, he said, "You're good." He jabbed his finger at his chest. "I'm good." He gestured toward the sleeping cats. "They're good. Satisfied?"

She wasn't. "If we're all good," she countered, "then who's evil?"

His smile faded. "I believe you mentioned something about a man in a quarry. Wouldn't you agree that he's evil?"

Inary drew in her breath, too dismayed to answer. As if upset by her distress, the cats both roused, trotted over to her and jumped into her lap. She glanced at Enkidu's missing paw and shuddered.

It was true the red-haired man might have been crazy. Or maladjusted. But, whether she wanted to admit to Ford that it existed or not, what she'd felt emanating from the man in the quarry had been pure evil.

CHAPTER FOUR

The next morning, as Inary fed the cats, she discovered that when she'd shopped in Sweetgrass she'd forgotten to stock up on more cans of cat food. This meant she'd have to drive into Norwich and buy some.

An hour later, as she edged her car along the sandy drive toward the road, she realized she was reluctant to go into the village and wondered why.

Her memories of Norwich were meager. Once she'd attended grade school in town during a spring when her father left her with Aunt Inary. Fourth grade. As she pulled onto the blacktop, she recalled her aunt walking up to this spot with her every weekday morning and waiting until little Inary boarded the school bus. She remembered few other details about that spring. Or about the village of Norwich.

She did know Norwich was an old mining and logging town. As she drove along the main street, Inary saw a few new false fronts hiding the ancient brick or frame buildings, but nothing could give the town a modern look. The numerous bars along the street—Swede's, Mike's, Babe's—were reminders of how the miners and lumberjacks had once spent their pay. She found a new barracklike supermarket by the old train depot, parked her car and went in.

Almost immediately she began to feel uneasy. If she glanced toward the other customers, none of them seemed to be looking at her, but when her back was turned she sensed their stares. And hostility.

March is too early for tourists, she told herself, so you're probably the only stranger in town. Naturally they're curious. You're imagining the dislike.

But after she stowed the bag of cat food in the car and slid behind the wheel, she shut the door with a sense of relief. She'd never been the paranoid type, imagining people were conspiring against her, but she couldn't dismiss her discomfort. No one had smiled or said hello, no one had spoken to her except the cashier and all she'd said was, "nine eighty-nine, please." Not even adding, as cashiers often did, "Have a nice day."

Inary's first impulse was to drive home as fast as possible but she quelled the notion, refusing to allow herself to be intimidated. So she drove the length of the main street slowly and deliberately. A Pasties sign in a café window caught her eye, bringing back memories of that delicious Upper Peninsula Cousin Jack specialty, the Cornish meat pie.

On impulse, she turned onto a side street, parked and went into the café. The teenage waitress who took her take-out pasty order showed a marked lack of interest in Inary, being too busy flirting with the one other customer in the café, a burly young man in a red plaid jacket.

As she waited for her order, Inary watched passersby through the window, wondering if she'd recognize anyone. It wasn't likely, since she hadn't made many friends in Norwich and eleven years had passed since she'd seen any of them. She couldn't even bring to mind their names. Except for one. And that name belonged to someone she definitely didn't want to meet again.

Of course, he'd probably left town long ago. As she recalled, he hadn't attended the local public schools but, since his family had money, had been sent to a private school somewhere in the east and no doubt had gone on to an Ivy League college. There'd be nothing in Norwich to lure him back permanently.

Carrying her pasty, she left the café, returned to her car and headed for home, still preoccupied with this unhappy remnant of her adolescence she thought she'd long-ago put behind her for good. As she waited at a Stop sign for her chance to cross the bridge over the Norwich River, a gleaming black foreign sports car drove past the intersection. She noticed the car first, then the driver.

Inary's breath caught. No! It couldn't be. She stared after the black car until the driver waiting behind her honked in exasperation. She shot ahead, over the bridge, and drove far too fast along the highway.

It hadn't been Roy Nuhaim in the sports car, she told herself firmly. She'd conjured up his image because she'd been thinking about him. At the moment she could visualize Roy's curly golden hair and his brilliant blue eyes as clearly as though he was seated next to her. She remembered him, oh yes, she remembered him all too well.

For no good reason. What happened back then wasn't important. What happened on Agate Point was not her fault—she'd been only fifteen and a total innocent.

Inary had been sure she'd filed the memory away permanently but it surfaced now, as vivid as the bright sunny day when she'd met Roy on her aunt's beach.

Not by prearrangement—she'd barely exchanged a dozen words with him in her life and she was far too shy to invite any boy to come and see her. Especially one as handsome as Roy—and older than she by at least three years....

Fifteen-year-old Inary was alone on the point, her favorite spot on her aunt's private beach. Here the trees hid her from view and, without fear of discovery, she could indulge her fondness for acting, could pretend to be anyone she chose, from a princess to an old-time Western dance-hall girl. Here was the best view of the Porcupine Mountains, rising rounded and gray-blue in the Western distance with the bright blue of the lake below. Here, too, on the pebbly beach, beautiful agates could be found.

She'd been searching for agates and was rising with a marvelous find clutched in her sandy fingers, when someone spoke.

"Hello, Inary." A boy's voice.

She whirled around and came face-to-face with Roy Nuhaim. Shocked, she could only stare. What was he doing here on the point?

As if in answer, he said, "I came to see you."

Tansy, who'd accompanied her to the point, fled into the woods, streaking away as though pursued by a dozen dogs. Inary, completely bemused by Roy, scarcely noticed the cat's departure. Flattered that he'd singled her out from all the other girls, she finally managed to mumble, "Hi, Roy."

He was so handsome with his hair gleaming golden in the sun, his jeans riding low on his hips and those clear blue eyes gazing at her. Gazing admiringly. She could hardly believe he wasn't a figment of her imagination.

"You've got the sexiest eyes I've ever seen," he said.

She swallowed. "Uh, they're just sort of hazel."

He shook his head. "They're the color of amber. A guy could get trapped in them and never be free."

Breathless with fascination, she watched him yank his T-shirt over his head, baring his chest. "Got to take advantage of the sun," he told her. "I see you are."

He reached toward her, his fingers caressing the bare skin between her two-piece bathing suit—not a bikini, Aunt Inary wouldn't let her wear one, but not completely old-fashioned, either. Goose bumps rose on Inary's arms from his touch. She tried not to stare at the wisps of golden hair between his nipples, more because his partial nakedness made her feel a little scared than because she worried about being polite.

And then—Then what? What had happened after that? If she'd recalled everything up until that moment, why was the rest of that afternoon jumbled in her mind, cut into bits and pieces that made no sense? As she struggled to fit the pieces together, she felt herself begin to drift and, with effort, pushed Roy and the past firmly from her mind.

"Damn!" Inary cried, slamming on the brakes. She'd missed her turnoff. Worse, she'd been in danger of slipping into one of her spells while driving the car. That had never happened before and might have been disastrous.

Should she up her dosage of medicine? She hated to without discussing an increase with her doctor. But he was in California. Not that she couldn't call him. Somehow, though, she was reluctant to reconnect herself to anyone she knew in California, even by a phone call.

The cats came running when she got out of the car. She noted with surprise and pleasure that Enkidu, though he still trailed behind Gilgamesh, was much less awkward. Apparently he was adjusting to being on three instead of four legs, as the vet had assured her he would.

Later in the morning, finding herself too restless to stay inside, she bundled up and went out with the cats. On the beach, an icy wind swept across the rough lake, chilling her to the bone, and so she plunged into the woods to escape from the cold. Though the trees did offer protection against the wind, the woods held their own damp chill.

She came to a pond whose brown water lay quiescent, and she stopped, looking about. The soggy ground underfoot, as well as the spruce and hemlock surrounding her, warned her she was entering the swamp she knew lay to the west of the property. In a week or two or three, frog choruses would be singing here, announcing spring's belated arrival. As the weather warmed, algae would grow in the stagnant water, turning the pond a bright green. Its surface would skitter with insect life and, alas, its depths would produce mosquitoes.

Turning back, she spotted a barely perceptible trail leading away from the pond and began to follow it. Gilgamesh darted ahead of her and vanished between the trees. There was no sign of Enkidu. She heard the faint sound of music—Dixieland—and realized she must be somewhere behind Ford's house. Evidently he was taking today off, too.

Moments later the trees thinned, the path ended, and she found herself gazing at Ford's back door. Both Enkidu and Gilgamesh sat on the stoop waiting for her as if they'd expected this was her destination all along.

"Come on, you guys, we're going home," she told them.

Neither cat budged. She scowled at them. "You don't live here and you know it. Come on, now."

They continued to ignore her. Exasperated, she strode to the stoop, meaning to pick up Enkidu and carry him, trusting that Gilgamesh would then follow. At that moment Ford opened the back door. Warm air rushed to meet her, plus a trumpet riff that could only be Al Hirt's.

"Welcome," Ford said.

Flustered, not wanting him to think she intended to camp on his doorstep, Inary muttered, "The cats lured me here."

By this time both cats had eased past him into the house. He gestured for her to enter.

"Just long enough to corral my—" she began.

"I was hoping you might drop by." He smiled at her, a genuine smile that lingered in his usually somber eyes.

"I wasn't planning to."

"Didn't I say to always trust your cats?" he asked as he closed the door and ushered her from the tiny storm shed into the kitchen.

"Trust them to lead me astray, is more like it."

"Never! They only want what's best for you."

"And coming to see you is best for me?"

"Actually, yes. I'm one person you can be certain means you no harm."

His words reminded Inary of the cold shoulder she'd gotten in Norwich earlier and she told him about it. "I doubt if any one of them could have recognized me," she finished. "Do they behave like that to all strangers?"

He waved her toward the stool at the counter and started the coffeemaker. "Small towns thrive on gossip. The word is out that Miss Cameron's niece from California is living in her house on the lake. They saw your license plate, put two and two together and identified you."

"Maybe they did deduce who I was. But that doesn't explain why they snubbed me."

He leaned against the wall, studying her. "You were a child when you stayed here with your aunt, so you'd have seen her from a child's point of view. While it's true children often find adult behavior inexplicable, did she ever strike you as being odder than most adults?"

Inary thought it over. "I can't be sure," she said finally. "The trouble is, my father always warned me to ignore what he referred to as his sister's 'peculiar habits.' So I guess I pretty much did." She smiled at a recollection. "Actually, I thought it was fun rather than weird to gather rose petals with her under the full moon because, as she insisted, that was the proper time. They were for the sachets she made."

"In her later years, at least," Ford continued, "the residents of Norwich came to regard Miss Cameron as more than peculiar. Many of them believed she was crazy and a fair percentage called her a 'crazy old witch.'"

Inary stared at him in surprise. "You said she wasn't crazy."

"That's true, she wasn't. But I imagine her behavior seemed wildly eccentric to them. And, of course, she *was* a witch."

Inary blinked, uncertain she'd heard him right. "Did you say—?" she began.

"Miss Cameron was a witch? Yes. It runs in the female line of the family, or so she told me."

Was this in line with that mumbo jumbo he'd thrown at her when she first arrived? Something about inheriting her aunt's gift? Witchcraft—was that the gift? How ridiculous. Hilarious, even.

Yet, somehow she found it scary rather than funny. Was Ford out of his mind? Many nurses insisted all shrinks were a bit off, that they were attracted to their specialty in the first place because they were somewhat skewed. Or needed help.

He smiled wryly. "I see I've startled you. And I can tell that you don't believe in witches."

"I believe some people *think* they're witches," she said, choosing her words carefully. "And others *pretend* to be witches, usually for unscrupulous reasons."

"What you say is quite true. But you miss the point. Some people really do have unusual powers and *are* witches. Your aunt was one of them. And so some of the villagers are wary of you. Who knows, you may have inherited the same abilities."

"*I* know I didn't," she snapped.

"But they don't. So some of them are unfriendly."

"It's hard to accept what you've said."

He shrugged. "You asked, I told you." He turned away to pour the coffee.

Inary watched him, noticing how he seemed to move in time to the beat of the jazz, easy and graceful despite his stocky build. He wasn't cover-boy handsome in the way Roy Nuhaim had been, but he was definitely attractive, no woman would deny that.

Damn, she hadn't meant to let Roy creep into her mind again. She didn't want to believe it could have been Roy she'd seen in the village.

As she stirred cream into her coffee she said casually, "You seem to be acquainted in Norwich. Have you met anyone there by the name of Roy Nuhaim?"

Inary felt rather than saw him stiffen. He spooned sugar into his cup before saying, "As far as I know, he doesn't live in Norwich."

A tricky answer, but what else could you expect from a shrink? She'd have to be blunter. "Do you know Roy?"

"I've been told Nuhaim's a lawyer practicing in Ironwood."

Ironwood. Seventy miles away from Norwich. Too close, as far as she was concerned. Still, since Roy didn't actually live in the village, chances are they'd never meet. And, anyway, why was she so concerned? She was no longer fifteen, no longer so pitifully naive.

"Evidently you've met Nuhaim," Ford said.

"Many years ago," she said hastily. "We were never really friends."

"Then why ask about him?"

"I thought I might have seen him in Norwich, and it startled me. I assumed he'd left town years ago." Which was the truth. She looked up and met his narrowed gaze.

What was he thinking? That she wanted to see Roy again? Nothing could be farther from the truth. She dreaded meeting him. If only she could recall exactly what had happened between Roy and her on the point. She found it strange that part of her memory of that time was so clear, while the rest remained out of focus. Why? Had she suffered one of her spells then, was that it?

Spell or not, she remembered all too well how it had ended.

"I took a walk to Agate Point earlier," Ford said.

His remark startled her until she decided he couldn't know about the past, about Roy, so he must simply be changing the subject.

"Without getting dunked in the creek?" Her voice was a tad too bright.

"No dunking. But I did find an agate on the beach there that I think is rather remarkable." He fished in the pocket of his jeans and produced a walnut-sized agate with clear white rings in the warm brown of the stone.

"How lovely. It's one of the nicest I've ever seen." Inary reached for the agate, but as her hand closed over it, everything spun around her, Ford and his kitchen slipped away into the mist, and she found herself fifteen again, back on Agate Point with Roy Nuhaim....

Roy leaned toward her. To kiss her? Her anticipation was laced with fear—boys her own age had kissed her, but Roy was older. Experienced. She wasn't. Not knowing exactly what to expect, not certain what she really wanted, she took a step backward and thrust her hand between them, holding out the agate she'd just found like an offering.

"Isn't this beautiful?" she asked breathlessly.

He glanced from her face to the agate and back. "Beautiful," he murmured, his blue eyes alight with an emotion she wasn't sure she understood. Or liked.

Flustered, she said, "You can have the agate if you want."

He smiled. "You're positive you want to give it to me?"

"Oh, yes, the agate's yours."

His fingers stroked her palm as he took the stone from her. At the same time he said something soft and low, words she didn't understand. He continued murmuring while he tucked the agate away in his back pocket.

Was it the words that made her feel so strange?

And then, without warning, he pulled her into his arms and his mouth came down hard on hers. His hands moved over her body, touching her breasts, cupping her buttocks, pressing her against him. For a brief instant she felt trapped, and then her mind went blank.

She became pure sensation, pure feeling. She didn't object when he yanked off her swimsuit bra and caressed her bare breasts. She wanted what Roy wanted, he made her want him. At the same time, she was vaguely aware that a tiny part of her watched in anguished but helpless distress as Roy eased her to the pebble-strewn sand.

At that moment she would have done anything for Roy, but suddenly her aunt stood over them, chanting in a wild singsong that drove Roy to his feet, staring at her aunt, who pointed at him as she intoned.

With a muttered curse, Roy backed away, grabbed his T-shirt and fled....

Warm arms held her; a man's voice spoke soothingly in her ear. Roy? Her heart pounding, Inary tried to struggle free.

"It's all right," the man said. "You're safe with me." Ford's voice, not Roy's.

Inary gathered her wits. She was twenty-six, not fifteen. She was in Ford's house, not on the point, in Ford's arms, not Roy's.

She'd recovered her lost memories of what had happened between her and Roy. Recovered them during another of her spells.

Embarrassed, she pulled away from Ford, mumbling, "I'm all right now."

"Was it a vision of the past or the future this time?" he asked, helping her back onto the stool.

She grimaced. "The past," she said without thinking, then was immediately sorry she'd revealed even that much.

"Don't be upset," he advised. "It may be that coming back here is triggering these visions, reminding you of episodes you need to remember. Like the door in the attic."

Inary sighed. He had no idea how painful it was to recall her humiliation as she crouched half-naked on the pebbly beach with her aunt standing over her.

"His kind isn't for you," Aunt Inary had warned. "He doesn't care for you—his only intent was to destroy." Her words held sadness, not contempt.

But Inary despised herself because she knew the words were true. Roy cared nothing for her, and yet she'd been ready to give herself away without even the lie of love between them.

It was small comfort now to know she'd never made the same mistake again.

What upset her even more was that she'd had another spell so soon after her last. And in front of Ford. Belatedly she realized he'd spoken of visions. She forced herself to look at him.

"Visions?" she asked.

He frowned. "What else? This vision trance was briefer than the one you had in the attic. By holding you, I was able to keep you on your feet."

It warmed her to know he'd held her. Kept her safe. But it disturbed her that he knew about the spells, knew her weakness. She started to ask him why he referred to the spells as vision trances, then changed her mind, preferring not to discuss them with him, to keep her worries to herself.

Her California physician had warned her that an increasing incidence of the spells might push her into a vegetative fugue state—a bleak future. If she told Ford about her case, it was likely his prognosis would be equally gloomy—so why bother?

Appropriately enough, Pete Fountain's clarinet was soaring into the "St. James Infirmary Blues"—as far as she was concerned, the saddest blues of all. She blinked back tears, feeling sorrier for herself with each note.

The next she knew, Ford had grasped her hand, pulled her off the stool and wrapped his arms around her. "I can't bear seeing you look so unhappy," he murmured in her ear.

She nestled in this haven, feeling safe and protected. Nothing bad could happen; he'd keep her from harm. But gradually, almost imperceptibly, her feeling of warm security edged into something quite different. She became aware of the hard length of his body against her softer one, the whisper of his breath caressing her ear, sending a frisson of desire sliding along her spine.

She began to want more than the comfort of being held. Without considering what she was doing, she snuggled closer to him. His sharp intake of breath excited her and she raised her face to look at him.

For a moment she gazed into his unusual brown eyes, marveling at the different-sized golden wedges in his irises. Glowing eyes. Why had she ever thought of them as cold? His lips hovered over hers, making her edgy with anticipation. Slowly, oh, so slowly, he bent his head until his mouth grazed hers, the tip of his tongue tracing the outline of her lips.

Somebody moaned. Which of them was it? Lost in a yearning haze of need, she wasn't sure.

"We can't do this, Inary," he murmured against her lips. And then he kissed her.

CHAPTER FIVE

Ford's urgent kiss blazed through Inary, a flash fire whose flames destroyed all the barriers she'd so carefully erected during the years. An answering passion exploded deep inside her, blowing away caution and restraint.

She breathed in his scent, smoky and distinctive. As her lips parted, inviting invasion, she tasted his dark and dangerous flavor, one she would never forget. She wanted more of him, more and more and more. She wanted all of him.

And she knew he wanted her. She not only felt his arousal, she sensed and was excited by the hot demand that thrummed through him, threatening to drive him out of control. She yearned to give, she needed to take.

Give to this man, take from him. Only him.

With the tiny vestige of sanity that remained to her, she tried to curb her headlong rush of desire and managed to gasp against his lips, "Ford?"

He shuddered, his tremor shaking her, as well. Then he dropped his arms, stepped back, turned away from her and leaned against the wall as though needing its support.

"I forgot myself," he muttered. "You make it damn difficult for me."

She stared at him, bereft, confused and indignant.

Feeling tears threaten, she took a deep breath and let it out slowly, searching for composure, refusing to cry because of this man—or any man. "*I* make it difficult for you?" she asked, intending to point out with some tartness that she was certainly no more to blame than he was.

But Ford misinterpreted her choice of words. He turned to face her, lips twisted in a sardonic smile. "Echoing is *my* schtick—don't try to hoist a shrink by his own technique. But, yes, you do make it difficult. Every time I touch you I forget what my role is."

Inary drew herself up. "Your role? And just what do you mean by that?"

"I'm supposed to be protecting you."

She was incredulous. "Protecting me? Like some modern-day knight-errant? Against what, may I ask? And just why should you think I need protection?"

"Because, damn it, you've inherited the Cameron power and you don't have a clue how to go about using it."

"You can't mean you think *I'm* a witch!" she cried.

"What you are, you are. It has nothing to do with what I think or don't think. Whether you accept it or not, you do have power. Latent, at the moment, but shining clearly enough to be seen by anyone who has the ability. Power attracts power, Inary, including those who covet yours. Like the man in the quarry. Undoubtedly he saw the shining."

Inary hugged herself. "Don't talk about him."

"Your aunt should have told you when you were a child. She should have prepared you. She chose not to, and now it's up to me. And, damn it, I'm not the right person."

"I prefer not to believe a word of this," Inary said coldly.

"Then you'll face more danger than either of us can cope with."

"But I don't have any power!" she cried. "Nor do I want to have any."

"The choice isn't yours. You can't give power away, but those who covet what you have can subvert you and use your power for their selfish purposes."

"How do you know all this—this esoteric mumbo jumbo?"

"Because I'm a witch, too. Or warlock, as some might call me." His tone was somber.

"You must be crazy!"

He shook his head. "No such luck, Inary. What I'm telling you is the truth, and sooner or later you'll have to face it. You'll have to acknowledge that the safe and narrow little world you've tried to build around yourself is no protection against the danger your power attracts. You've already had your first lesson. In California."

"I don't care to discuss the subject any longer." Inary stalked into the living room, gathered up Enkidu from the hearth rug and, with the other cat trailing her, left by the front door, refraining with difficulty from slamming it behind her.

She hurried home, seething with fury. How dare Ford try to feed her such nonsense? Claiming to be a witch. Insisting she was a witch. Like her aunt. Attempting to scare her by mentioning the man in the quarry. She was inside her house before she remembered he'd also kissed her all but senseless. That made her even angrier.

I'll find that key to the attic room, she told herself. I'll unlock the door and prove to myself once and for all that everything I've heard from Ford Werlich is a lie. Because there'll be nothing evil in the room. How can there be?

Where could the key be hidden? She didn't intend to waste time rushing around looking in all the places Ford must have already searched. No, what she had to do was think back to her childhood and try to recall anything her aunt may have said to her about a key. First, though, she had to calm down, she had to order her mind.

She threw a log on the fire and poked it up a little, then settled herself in her aunt's wingback rocker beside the fireplace. Both cats leaped onto her lap, curled up and began purring. She settled into the chair, rocking gently, seeking to blank her mind as she watched the dancing flames. After a time, she began to remember one long-ago afternoon when her aunt had sat rocking in this same chair with Tansy in her lap while the child Inary had sat on a footstool by the hearth.

"What would you do, child, if you came into the house and I wasn't here?" Aunt Inary had asked as rain pattered persistently, endlessly against the old gray house.

"I guess I'd wait for you," little Inary said.

"But if I still didn't come?"

"I don't know. Take care of Tansy and—" Her words had trailed off because she really didn't know what else to do.

Her aunt stopped rocking and leaned forward. "Listen to me, for this is important. If a whole day and night go by and I don't come back, here's what you must do." She rose, knelt on the rug in front of the hearth and motioned to little Inary to join her.

When child and woman knelt side by side, her aunt moved the iron owl that sat on the raised bricks of the hearth, setting it onto the rug. "Count up seven bricks and over three." Her aunt demonstrated, then removed a penknife from the pocket of her apron. "Take the point of a knife and ease this brick up.... See how it comes loose? There's a space under the brick—put your hand in and feel."

Nine-year-old Inary, wide-eyed, put her small hand into the opening left by the removal of the brick.

"This is where I'll leave a message if I must," her aunt had said. "This is where you'll find it. But you are never, ever to touch this brick under any other circumstances. I will punish you if you do. I trust you understand."

Inary had nodded then, just as she nodded now, all these years later. The occasion had never arisen to look for a message, because her aunt had always come back. But she no longer could. The dead did not return.

Inary eased the cats from her lap and rose. She dropped to her knees, shifted the iron owl and counted the bricks, prying the loose one up and out with the edge of the ash shovel. Thrusting her hand inside the cavity, she smiled in triumph. She'd found the key.

But a few minutes later, standing in the attic, looking from the locked door to the key in her hand, she began to have doubts. Ford had asked her to promise to let him know if she found the key, stressing the danger of opening the door. Should she put any credence in what he'd said? Inary shook her head. Like as not, it was part and parcel of his other witchcraft nonsense. Though she'd finally promised to let him know she'd found the key, she hadn't said *when* she'd tell him and she fully intended to look inside the room first.

Gilgamesh had insisted on being let out before she went upstairs, but Enkidu had followed her into the attic and stood next to her now, staring at the door, his fur raised.

She marched to the door, then hesitated again before inserting the key. Why was the cat uneasy? Why had Aunt Inary kept her out of this room, going so far as to hypnotize her into forgetting the room was there? Her aunt must have had a reason, but what could it be?

If she didn't unlock the door, she'd never know. Inary turned the key. Her fingers quivered on the knob, but she turned it, too, and pushed the door open, prepared for a musty, mildewed smell. Instead, a strange spicy odor wafted from the room. There was one window, covered with a dark blind. There was no light switch she could find within the room.

"I'll just take a quick glance around," she said to Enkidu, her words echoing unpleasantly in the dark. For some reason the light coming from behind her, through the attic skylight, didn't seem to penetrate into the room.

She'd go in and pull up the blind, that's what she'd do. Inary, denying her reluctance to enter the room, forced herself to step inside. She took one step. Two. As she took the next step, her right foot came down on something soft and she cried out, afraid Enkidu had followed her in and she'd stepped on him.

Twisting sideways, she lost her balance and stumbled. As she fell, she felt pressure against her throat, choking her, while something unseen brushed across her face. She tried to scream but could not. The spicy scent overpowered her, clogging her brain, sending her spinning, whirling into blackness....

The woman knew what she was risking. Yet what choice did she have? There was a young child to protect, the little girl who was her namesake, the child she loved but didn't dare to keep near her. How could he be so thoughtless, leaving the girl with her, leaving her here to gather danger?

If only he would take her away and watch over her carefully until she grew old enough to understand. If only that could happen. The woman sighed. Her brother, so many years younger than she, had never believed in the ageless workings of good and evil. He thought only of himself, of his own convenience.

Risky though it was to use this room, she must try, with her rose petals and her garlands of herbs and her special candles and her incantations to work a strong enough spell to protect the child and keep her safe until she grew into her power and learned to protect herself....

A voice called her name. A man's voice. Brightness cut through the darkness. He called her name again and again. "Inary. Inary." Called with the power to make her answer. She opened her eyes to find everything blurred.

Fingers touched her, smoothing the hair back from her forehead. Ford's face swam into her vision. She was lying on the floor and he was kneeling beside her. She stared at him in confusion. What had happened?

"You little fool," he muttered.

She heard his words, but they didn't make sense. She struggled to understand where she was. Who she was. An old woman? But, no, she wasn't old, she was young. And yet, only moments ago...

"I'm Inary Cameron," she whispered. "Myself. Not my aunt." But hadn't she been Aunt Inary, there in the darkness?

"What are you talking about?" Ford asked.

A rough tongue scraped her face. She turned her head and saw Enkidu.

"Are you all right?" Ford asked.

"I don't know," she said slowly. "Help me to sit up."

He helped her, holding her with an arm around her shoulders. Her head swam, and she leaned against him.

"I was my aunt," she said. "Not a dream. Inside her body, being an old woman, thinking her thoughts about me."

He shifted position, gathering her closer. "Don't be upset." His voice was low, soothing. "These things sometimes happen in visions."

Visions? Did he mean she'd had another spell? Inary looked around. She was in an unfamiliar room, a small room with one window where a torn black blind hung in tatters.

"The blind was nailed to the frame," Ford said. "I ripped it off."

The locked room. She'd found the key....

Enkidu brushed against her legs. Gilgamesh, she saw, stood in the doorway to the room. What was he doing in the house? Hadn't he been outside?

"How did you know I was here?" she asked Ford.

"Gilgamesh came to fetch me. He yowled on my doorstep until I opened the door. When I discovered he didn't want in, I knew something was wrong over here."

Inary stared at the cat. How had he known she needed help? Both cats had seen her find the key, and cats were intelligent creatures. But not *that* smart.

As if answering her unspoken question, Ford said, "How many times do I have to tell you the cats are trying to protect you? They recognize and respond to your power—and mine—even if you refuse to believe either of us has any."

"They saw me find the key. But—"

"The key evidently is contaminated with some of this room's evil, and they sensed that. It's not a good idea for us to stay in here. Can you walk?"

Feeling better by the moment, she nodded. He helped her to her feet and, with an arm around her, led her toward the door. She stopped abruptly beside a crumpled red silk rug on the floor, a memory sequence flooding her mind. "This must be what I stepped on. I thought it was Enkidu, and I tripped and fell." She raised a hand to her neck. "I felt someone choking me."

Ford gestured toward a narrow rope festooned with dried plants that hung kitty-corner across the room. "You probably fell against that. What I don't understand is why you unlocked the door without letting me know you found the key. You promised—"

"No, I did not. You asked me to promise to tell you, and I told you I would. I made no other promise."

"Whatever. You knew damn well what I meant. Why do you keep refusing to recognize what's involved here?" He waved his hand around the room. "Do you know the meaning of any of this?"

"The herbs on the rope," she said, remembering. "When I was my aunt and worried about the child, I came in here to—to work some spell to keep her safe. Herbs and rose petals and special candles were part of it."

"The candles will be in the chest. With your aunt's other things." He nodded to a small wooden chest near the window.

"You said you'd never been in this room!"

"I haven't. Let's lock it up again and go downstairs."

"Why are you in such a hurry? All I can see is a small room, empty except for the herbs, the chest and a red rug on the floor. What's so sinister about that?"

"Have you looked under the rug?"

"Have you?" she countered.

"No, but I can tell you what's there. A pentacle."

"A what?"

He released her, crouched and flung the rug back.

Inary stared at an inlaid circle containing a five-pointed star, the wood of the inlays a curious reddish color. Faint unease woke in her. "A pentacle?" she asked.

He nodded curtly. "Sometimes called a pentagram. If drawn with one point up, it represents the light of the spirit hidden within."

Inary studied the red star. "From where we stand, looking toward the window," she said, "I see two points uppermost."

"Two points uppermost gives the pentacle a more sinister meaning, which I fear this one has. Notice the sorcerer's circle surrounding the star. Those who misuse their power might try to use this symbol to call up a dark force, hoping to enhance their ability to work evil.''

"My aunt wasn't evil!"

"Definitely not. I think something happened to her in this room, though, something terrifying enough that she banished its existence from your mind, locked the room and hid the key."

Remembering how she'd felt herself to be her aunt as she lay unconscious, Inary said, "I think maybe she might have tried to use the pentacle. I don't know how, but I think I do know *why*. To protect me—or, rather, the child I used to be."

Ford sighed. "She might have. These symbols of power are dangerously tempting. Unfortunately, too many things can go wrong."

Inary backed away from the pentacle. "I don't want any part of it."

Careful not to step on any part of the inlaid design, Ford retrieved the rug and covered the pentacle. Then he ushered her through the door into the attic proper where both cats waited, and he closed the door and locked it. He removed the key and offered it to her.

She shook her head. "You keep the key."

"No, the key should remain in the house. Put it back wherever you found it and don't tell me—or anyone—where the hiding place is. I don't think you'll be tempted to unlock the door again."

Inary accepted the key reluctantly, sliding it into her pocket. She didn't worry about being tempted to go into the room again—who would want to?—but she didn't like assuming responsibility for the key. Still, as Ford had made clear, it *was* her responsibility.

"You've confused and upset me with all this talk of witches and sorcerers and dark forces," she said. "I don't want to believe any of it."

"I don't blame you. But you have no choice. What we need to do is begin at the beginning. Downstairs."

When they were seated by the fire, with Enkidu in Ford's lap and Gilgamesh in hers, Ford said, "You begin. Tell me why you're here."

"Because Aunt Inary left me the house," she said.

"You've known that for three months. Why did you make the decision to come here to live rather than trying to sell the place?"

"I—I didn't like California."

"Why? Most people do."

Inary tensed, disturbing Gilgamesh, who eyed her reproachfully. She took a deep breath and stroked his fur, as much to soothe herself as to placate him. "I heard the night caller," she said, her voice barely above a whisper. "Before it happened, I thought he was only one of my aunt's stories. Not bedtime stories—these were scary tales, maybe too scary for a child, but she told them to me, anyway." She couldn't make herself go on.

"I'm not a patient man," he said after a few minutes of silence. She heard the tightness of suppressed emotion in his voice.

"I have a hard time talking about what happened. Let me tell you my aunt's story first. When I was a little girl, we'd hear the owls hooting as they hunted at night and she'd say, 'Listen. Listen well, child, for you must learn to recognize the owl. His voice is clear and lonely. An owl is nothing to fear, except the white owl, because a white owl can mean death.

" 'Other birds call in the night—you've heard the whippoorwill's desolate cry often enough. But something more deadly than a bird or an animal also calls in the night, beckoning in the dark, coaxing you with whispers, soft sounds to bind you to him before you realize you're listening. I hope you never hear him, child. But he exists. And he calls at night, though I have yet to hear him.' "

"Your aunt spoke the truth. There are no night callers here. Yet. How did one cross your path in California?"

Inary swallowed. "It all started when I took a trip to the Sierra foothills with my apartment mate and her fiancé. The snows were melting up higher on the peaks and the water gurgled and rushed in all the mountain streams. We came on a deserted granite quarry, and I was the one who found this strange level slab of granite with the hollow in the center, a hollow where rust-colored splotches stained the black-and-white rock...."

"Blood," Inary had said to Joanne, who laughed and walked on with George toward the stream.

Inary tried to follow, but the stone fascinated her, drawing her back. On impulse, she climbed onto the rock and discovered her body just fit into the hollow.

"Offering yourself up?" Joanne called to her.

She knew her friend was teasing, but the idea made her so uncomfortable she slid off the rock hurriedly and joined the other two at the stream.

After they'd eaten lunch, Inary had taken a walk so that George and Joanne could have some privacy. To her dismay, even though she'd meant to go in the opposite direction, her steps led her back to the stone slab. Worse, she felt compelled to climb onto it again and lie in the hollow. A part of her, repelled by the rusty spots and a faint, rank odor she hadn't noticed before, struggled not to obey. But, in the end, she'd settled into the hollow and fallen asleep in that unlikely place. Or, perhaps, she'd had one of her spells. In any case, she dreamed.

Fires ringed the rock, voices chanted, a flame rose up, up and over her, in its center a man with fiery hair, a man with a golden knife. The naked man, flames licking around him, lifted the knife.

Terror-stricken, unable to move, she closed her eyes as the knife blade plunged down, down....

A hand gripped her arm, shaking her, and she screamed and sat up. Joanne was kneeling on the slab beside her, no laughter in her eyes now.

"I couldn't rouse you," she said. "You scared me to death. What in God's name are you doing here, of all places?"

Inary paused in her retelling, conscious of Ford's intent regard, aware she still had no answer as to why she'd gone back to the granite slab.

"I wasn't hurt," she told Ford. "But when I brushed my hair that night I found a piece of my hair missing. Cut. I never did tell Joanne. But I began to have nightmares and walk in my sleep. Joanne would find me wandering in the living room with Gilgamesh trailing after me. And then she got married and left."

"Leaving you alone."

"I had Gilgamesh and, later, Enkidu. I think the cats heard the whispers when they began, when the night caller tried to—to—" she couldn't go on.

"To make you come to him," Ford finished. "Yes, the cats would hear. And do what they could to stop you. That's why he tried to dispose of them. The night caller had something of yours or you wouldn't have heard him."

Inary's hand went involuntarily to her hair. Ford set Enkidu onto the floor, rose and came to her, pushing aside strands of her hair until he found the missing lock.

Inary looked up at him, refusing to admit to herself how his touch made her tingle. "The night caller used some of my hair to hang Enkidu's amputated paw to my door," she said sadly. "After that I was afraid for the cats, as well as for myself, and so I bolted. Ran here."

"A smart move. Night callers derive their power from their own surroundings. He could follow you here, but since he wouldn't have any hold over you because he'd be powerless here, why should he? You're safe from him, Inary."

Noticing a single long gold-brown hair—hers—clinging to the sleeve of Ford's black sweatshirt, Inary plucked it off. Without considering what she was doing, or why, she leaned forward and dropped the hair into the fire. Disturbed, Gilgamesh leaped from her lap.

Ford leaned against the mantel, smiling approvingly. "That's right. Don't take chances."

She rose from her chair. "You believe me," she said, no question in her voice.

"Of course. Didn't I warn you that power attracts power?"

"You don't think I hallucinated?"

"No. Strange and terrifying things really did happen to you. And since they did, why have you been so reluctant to accept what I've been trying to tell you?"

"I don't want to accept it!" she cried. "I don't want to have power, to attract horrible creatures like night callers."

"When did you first start believing in bacteria?" he asked.

She blinked. "What?"

"You know, germs."

"Why—I suppose in grade school, in those health classes where they teach you about washing hands and all."

"In other words, you didn't wait to see your first microbe under the microscope before you accepted that it existed."

"No. I mean, I was taught. The books said—"

"So you didn't need proof. How about atoms?"

"Oh, all right, I've never seen an atom but, yes, I'm convinced they exist."

"Then believe me," Ford said. "What you've already been through ought to be some evidence in my favor. Try to accept what you are before worse happens to you."

"What do you mean worse? You said there weren't any night callers here."

"That's right. But night callers aren't the only ones with dark power. They aren't the only ones who may try to use what you have, to deprive you of what's rightfully yours and to destroy you in the process."

She stared at him. "Kill me, you mean?"

"You might survive. But you wouldn't want to."

CHAPTER SIX

That night, shaken by what Ford had told her, Inary had difficulty sleeping. Though upset by his announcement that he was a witch and that she had inherited her aunt's witch power, what disturbed her most at the moment was the worry over the increasing frequency of her spells.

Ford had called her spells "visions," but that was part and parcel of his witchcraft beliefs, so she didn't take him seriously. She hadn't begun having the spells until she was twelve, living in California with her father and her stepmother, Harriet. Since no physician had been able to successfully diagnose and treat Inary, Harriet, behind her father's back, had taken Inary to a wide variety of faith healers and self-proclaimed psychics.

None of them had helped. Her bizarre experiences with some of the healers had caused Inary to mistrust anyone who claimed supernormal abilities, but Harriet was ever optimistic. Too optimistic.

If she and my father hadn't separated when I was fifteen, Inary thought, Harriet would undoubtedly have consulted every offbeat practitioner from Santa Rosa to San Diego.

But Harriet had meant well, and Inary had never blamed her for trying to help.

The doctor Inary herself had finally chosen was a Fresno neurologist whose eventual diagnosis, a tentative one arrived at after many tests, was that she had an aberrant type of epilepsy. He'd decided this because her electroencephalograms consistently showed odd wave patterns that he was unable to otherwise explain. Dr. Janowicz had put her on medication after discussing the problem with her and warning her that it was possible she might eventually worsen and slip into what he called a fugue state where she'd be unable to function.

At first she'd thought the medication was helping, but since she'd come to Michigan, the spells had increased alarmingly.

She'd been on the verge of discussing her problem with Ford, but after what he'd said today, she'd drawn back. He might be a psychiatrist, but how could she trust a doctor who claimed he was a witch?

Tomorrow afternoon she began working at Sweetgrass and she couldn't afford to have anything go wrong there. Inary made up her mind to call Dr. Janowicz before she went to work.

That decided, she relaxed, believing she'd be able to sleep. But then, against her will, she found herself reliving those delicious passion-filled minutes in Ford's arms. It hurt to realize he'd been the one to pull away. What was the matter with her? After that stupid mistake she'd made at fifteen, she'd vowed never to lose control with a man. Until today, she never had.

Perhaps she would have come to her senses and drawn back, but Ford hadn't given her the opportunity to find out. What did he mean, he had to protect her? Against what? Against who? People around here seemed inclined to avoid her rather than menace her.

Witches! They didn't really exist.

Still, she couldn't dismiss the California night caller nor deny he'd held some strange power over her. Thank heaven she was now thousands of miles away from that danger. Yet her experience with him proved she didn't know everything, so it was possible she could be wrong about witches. Remotely possible. But even if they did exist, *she* certainly wasn't one.

When she finally did fall asleep, she dreamed she was on the beach at the point, searching through the stones to find an agate. Not just any agate, but one particular stone, the agate she'd found here once before and then lost. If she didn't find that lost agate something terrible was going to happen. So she searched and searched and searched and all in vain....

When the cats woke her in the morning, demanding to be let out, she was glad to escape from her frustrating dream.

After lunch she called Dr. Janowicz's office in California.

"I'm so sorry, Ms. Cameron," the receptionist told her, "but the doctor has taken a two-month leave of absence. He's traveling in Europe and won't return until the first of June. I can ask his associate to—"

"No, never mind." Inary thanked her and hung up. Since she'd never been seen by the associate, she didn't feel confident he could be any help to a strange patient, especially long distance. Feeling depressed, she put on her uniform, made certain the cats were inside and left for Sweetgrass.

I won't be nervous, Inary assured herself as she drove to the hospital. I'm working with children and I like children.

But when she was standing outside the locked door of C2, ready to insert the shiny new key the nursing office had given her, she took a deep breath to steady herself, fearing a repeat of the onslaught she'd gone through when she'd toured the unit.

They were waiting inside the door, all the faces, the hands. She braced herself as she started down the corridor. Voices babbled to her, but oddly, she thought, the children drew back as she passed. Not one of them touched her. What was wrong?

"They think you're the shot nurse," a small, older nurse assistant told her. "It's the black band on your cap. I'm Mary Johnson. You must be Ms. Cameron. We heard you were going to work evenings with us. I'll take you along to Ms. Wiitala—she's day charge."

As she led the way, Mary Johnson put her arm around one of the children. "This is Rocky," she said. "He's our helper."

Under a plastic helmet with the Detroit Lions logo, the boy's slack face worked into a smile. He was about nine, Inary thought, feeling a certain empathy for him because the protective helmet suggested he was an epileptic, subject to sudden, uncontrollable seizures that could make him fall.

"Hello, Rocky," she said warmly.

"Hi nurse, hi nurse, hi nurse, hi—"

His litany was interrupted by Ms. Wiitala, who adroitly avoided all patient contact as she fielded Inary into the nurses' station, shutting the half door to close them in.

"May I make a suggestion?" she asked. At Inary's nod, she added, "We're sort of informal here, so don't bother to wear your cap to work. Sooner or later one of the kids'll just yank it off and scrunch it up, anyway."

"Thanks for the tip," Inary said.

"Everyone calls me Wheatie," the day nurse said.

"I'm Inary."

After they'd counted the controlled drugs and signed the book, Wheatie gave Inary a quick orientation, showing her where things were at the nurses' station. "We had a real quiet day," she said. "Patient count remains at thirty-two. I'll run through the report with you, but there's nothing urgent going down."

When she finished, Wheatie added, "If you need to know anything else, ask your NAs. They've both been here for ages. See you." And she was gone.

Inary familiarized herself with her patients as she passed out the afternoon medications. Her first problem came when Sammy, a four-year-old blond boy given to sucking his fingers, vomited his medicine almost as soon as she'd coaxed it down him.

As Inary tried to decide whether to repeat the full dosage, Mary Johnson spoke up. "If Sammy doesn't get his tranquilizer, he climbs the walls all night. You ought to see him."

When Inary tried to give him another dose, Sammy spit the medicine up almost as fast as he'd swallowed it. Had he kept any down? She was afraid to give him more for fear he might get an overdose. Hoping for the best, she went on to the next child, a girl of about five or six named Sunny. She wore what looked like a catcher's mask.

"You don't have to take that off," Mary Johnson advised. "Best not to, anyway. Sunny'll take her medicine through a straw."

Which proved to be true.

"Why must Sunny wear that mask?" Inary asked once the girl ambled away from them.

"She bites. Herself. The nurses. Other patients. We used to have to keep her restrained, until Dr. Werlich tried putting that mask on her. It works great, and so far she hasn't figured out how to take it off. Makes me think that doctor isn't so bad, after all, no matter what they say."

Inary wondered what Mary meant about Ford not being "so bad." Every hospital had its grapevine, passing along rumors and gossip from one unit to another. What was the gossip about Ford? New as she was, she didn't think it was a good idea to ask, because people tended to be closemouthed when newcomers asked questions. Sooner or later, she was sure, someone would tell her.

She'd almost forgotten about the little girl she'd noticed in the corner the first day she toured the unit. But when she found the child sitting under the table in the dayroom, peering through her tangled dark hair, Inary immediately recalled the strange feeling she'd had at that time, the feeling that the little girl needed her.

Inary sat on the floor. She'd already learned that many of the children not only knew their names but could say them, so she said, "Hello, my name's Inary. What's yours?"

The child didn't reply, didn't respond in any way. Because she'd gone over the C2 patient list and, with the help of the children's wrist-band IDs and the aid of the NAs, identified all the other patients, Inary knew the little girl had to be Dorothy Marten. She was about to say so to the child, but changed her mind.

"I know someone who has a special name for you," she said instead. "Only special people get special names, so you must be one of them."

The girl lifted a hand to her hair, parting the strands slightly as though to see Inary better.

"He told me he calls you Mouse," Inary said. "Do you like that name?"

Not expecting anything much, she was surprised when the child raised her head, pushing her hair from her face, and stared. At the same time, Ford's image filled Inary's mind. Without thinking, she nodded. "Yes, Dr. Werlich's the one who told me."

Belatedly realizing what had happened and alarmed by her own response, Inary was about to backtrack when Mouse smiled, scooted over to her and touched her arm with a grimy little hand. Inary felt a strange sensation, as though something had brushed gently against her mind. Goose bumps rose on her arms, but before she could quite capture the eerie feeling, it was gone. So was Mouse's hand.

Mouse didn't retreat under the table again. Instead, she followed Inary on her rounds, though maintaining a certain distance between them, keeping beyond easy reach.

Ms. Beech, who hadn't spoken more than two words to Inary up until then, noticed. "Looks like Dorothy's taken to you," she said later, as she and Inary sat charting in the nurses' station. "I never saw her follow anyone before, except when Dr. Werlich comes on the unit. 'Course, not even he can get her to talk. She never says a word."

"Maybe she can't," Inary said, though she hadn't yet read through Mouse's chart, so she wasn't certain of her diagnosis.

"She ain't no deaf-mute," Ms. Beech said.

Although there were other reasons for muteness, Inary didn't list them. Mary Johnson had seemed to accept her right away but Ms. Beech hadn't. Not yet. Inary had met and worked with similar show-me-a-reason-to-respect-you NAs and nurses and had learned to tread warily with them at first.

"You met Dr. Werlich yet?" Ms. Beech asked.

Inary nodded.

"He's a strange one. For a while he used to take little Dorothy into the exam room every time he came over to C2. I watched him on the sly in case he was one of them real nutty shrinks you read about, but all he ever did was to sit her on the exam table and hold both her hands in his. Nothing wrong with that, I suppose, but it gave me the willies, somehow. Like they was talking without words, you know? Then all of a sudden he stopped. Hardly ever comes over here now, at least on evenings."

Though Ms. Beech's observation about talking without words upset Inary, she felt obliged to defend Ford. After all, he hadn't done anything wrong. "Maybe the doctor was conducting some kind of test," she said. "Didn't he write anything on her chart?"

Ms. Beech shook her head. "Not a word." She leaned closer. "I heard rumors about him from where he worked before, downstate, something about a patient who died and it was the doctor's fault. So I plan to keep right on watching."

Mary Johnson came into the station. "You best go see to Goldie," she said to Ms. Beech. "He's been painting again."

Ms. Beech rolled her eyes. "That boy'll be the death of me." She levered herself up and left the station.

"Painting?" Inary asked.

Mary grinned. "That's what we call it when one of the kids has a BM and his diaper isn't fastened tight enough. They're like babies, most of them, so they play with it. If one of us doesn't see what they're doing quick enough, there's a real mess."

Inary raised her eyebrows. "I can believe that."

"I'd have cleaned Goldie up but he's her favorite and she wouldn't like me taking care of him instead of her. You can't help getting attached to these kids. Rocky, now, he's my pet. Pretty soon you'll have a favorite of your own, wait and see. That is, if you stay on."

"Do you mean you think I'll be transferred to another unit?"

Mary shook her head. "Not exactly. No offense meant, but we've had more than one RN start here who just couldn't take the kids. They *are* kind of messy and all, but they can't help being that way. Really, they're sweethearts."

Inary didn't argue. Hadn't she been telling herself they were children like any others? Now all she had to do was convince herself it was true. And she would. She'd never been a quitter and she didn't plan to begin now.

What was she to make of Ms. Beech's remark about Ford's questionable past in another hospital? Obviously the NA was merely quoting what she'd heard through the grapevine. Though Inary realized how a small incident could be blown out of proportion as it passed from person to person, there was usually a kernel of truth embedded in every rumor. What, she wondered, had Ford done in that downstate hospital? Had he transferred to Sweetgrass to escape?

She no longer knew what to believe about Ford, her aunt or even herself.

Driving home shortly before midnight, she decided with some relief that she'd be able to adjust to her new job more easily than she'd feared. She was also pleased she hadn't been plagued with another of her spells.

As she pulled into her narrow drive, the glow from Ford's windows was welcome—especially since she'd forgotten to switch on a light in her own house before she left for work. She had to leave her car headlights on so she could see to unlock the front door.

As she opened the door, Gilgamesh shot out, with Enkidu close behind him. Inary sighed, hoping they'd return when she called them.

The faint fragrance of roses greeted her, as always. "The smell of roses must always be in the house," Aunt Inary used to say. "Never allow the sweet scent to fade lest good fortune fade with it."

As Inary poured milk into a pan, planning to have a cup of hot cocoa while she waited for the cats to be ready to come in, her mind drifted to the July nights when she and her aunt had gathered the pink petals of sweet briar, the wild roses, under the full moon. This year she'd harvest the scent of roses alone.

Spring came late up here, and summer even later. But, as she remembered, by May the lilacs were in bloom. There were violets then, too, purple by the streams where the wild flags grew, and yellow in the meadows, vying with the buttercups.

She drank her cocoa, called the cats in, then all three of them curled up on the bed and slept soundly.

* * *

Inary woke to a rainy morning. Gilgamesh, as usual, blamed her for the rain, grumbling at her when he eased through the shed door into the wet day.

"What do you think I am?" she asked him. "Even if I *was* a witch I couldn't stop the rain."

Enkidu, who also hated rain but didn't expect her to work marvels, slunk unhappily after Gilgamesh.

Remembering that it was the first of April, she called after the cats, "April showers bring May flowers." Actually, she didn't mind the rain since she had to work, anyway.

She'd be on duty over the weekend, then would begin her orientation on Monday, going to work an hour early until she completed her required fifteen hours of paid class time. Her days off were Thursday and Friday.

Because she knew that Ford, being a doctor, must have Saturdays and Sundays off, she wondered if she'd see him before she left for work today. Not that she wanted to. Or needed to.

But he didn't appear before it was time for her to go. She drove to Sweetgrass, telling herself it didn't matter, that she certainly didn't care.

She unlocked the door to C2 and found the children waiting for her. They weren't so shy today, either because they recognized her or because she'd left her black-banded cap home.

"Nurse, nurse," some called. Others said, as they did to all women, "Hi mama, hi mama!" The rest mumbled unintelligibly as they escorted her to the nurses' station.

After Wheatie finished the change-of-shift report, she said to Inary, "Didn't you say you lived in Norwich?'' At Inary's nod, she added, ''I see by the April schedule that you've got next Friday off. Some of us gals are going to a fish fry that night at Spurwood Lodge—it's just a couple of miles outside Norwich on the way to Bruce's Crossing. Want to join us?''

''Thanks,'' Inary said, pleased to be asked. ''I'd like to.''

''Meet you there at six-thirty—okay?''

''Right.''

The early evening went smoothly. Later, after all thirty-two children had been fed and washed and put to bed, Inary and Mary sat down to chart while Ms. Beech—''Call me Erma'' she'd told Inary—folded the clean clothes the laundry had delivered earlier.

''Dorothy's out of bed,'' Erma called from the linen closet. ''You want me to put her back?''

''No, I will,'' Inary replied, knowing Erma meant Mouse. Setting aside the chart she was working on, she left the station.

Mouse stood in the corridor, staring at the unit's locked door. Before she reached the girl, Inary heard a key being inserted from the other side, announcing the arrival of a visitor. Probably, she decided, the hospital's evening nursing supervisor making his rounds.

Inary wasn't at all prepared to see Ford Werlich step into the unit. Obviously Mouse was, though, because she smiled and hurried to take his hand.

Somehow Mouse could tell he was coming, Inary thought with an inner chill. That's what she was doing here—waiting for him.

Ford nodded to Inary before scooping Mouse up into his arms. ''Hey,'' he told the little girl, ''you belong in bed. I'll tuck you in, but then you'll have to stay there."

Inary watched him carry Mouse to the room she shared with three other girls, and then started back to the nurses' station. Before she reached it, a shriek froze her in place.

"That's Goldie!" Erma cried, running toward his room.

Inary hurried after her, Mary in her wake. In Goldie's six-crib room, she found the three-year-old boy sitting up, wailing bitterly, his right foot thrust between the bars of his crib. Blood oozed from a wound on the foot. Erma put down the crib side and lifted Goldie into her arms, cuddling him close as she tried to soothe him.

"What's wrong?" Ford asked as he entered the room.

Inary, examining the circular wound, said, "It looks like a bite."

"Oh, oh," Mary said. "Sunny must be loose. I'll go check on her."

"Bring Goldie to the exam room and I'll take a look at that foot," Ford ordered.

Fortunately, the bite was superficial and required only cleansing, antibiotic cream and a small dressing.

"Have the day shift notify his unit doctor," Ford said, "and keep a close watch for infection. The human mouth is loaded with potentially harmful bacteria."

While Erma returned Goldie to his crib, Inary went to Sunny's room, where Mary was retying Sunny's vest restraint. Since the mask came off at night, restraining her was the only feasible way to keep Sunny from harming herself or others during those hours.

"I found her in the dayroom," Mary said. "Lucky for us all she didn't decide to do any more damage."

Not wanting anything else to go wrong, Inary made a point of doing a patient-by-patient bed check. Rocky, she saw as she entered his room, slept with his helmet in the corner of his railed bed. He really did love that Lions helmet. Noting his arched body, she frowned and bent over him. As she feared, he was in tonic contracture, having a grand mal seizure.

Inary switched the light over the bed from dim to bright. His lips were cyanotic, blue in color. His teeth were clenched too tightly to insert any padding, so all she did was turn him onto his side to prevent him from choking on his own saliva while she waited for the seizure to end. Alarmed when minute after minute passed and he remained in contracture, she called, "Dr. Werlich!" as she pulled an oxygen mask over Rocky's face and turned on the wall oxygen unit.

Ford dashed into the room, took one look and said, "Check his chart and bring me the medication his unit doctor has ordered for status epilepticus."

In Rocky's case it was phenobarb rather than diazepam, and almost immediately after Ford had injected the drug into the boy's veins, Rocky stopped spasming and relaxed. Both Inary and Ford remained at the bedside for a time watching the sleeping boy in case he began having another seizure.

Mary stepped hesitantly into the room. "Is Rocky okay now?" she asked. When Inary nodded, Mary said, "He'll need his diapers changed. I'll do that and then sit by the bed and watch him if you want. I've done it before so I know what to look for."

At the nurses' station, Ford made a few notes on Goldie's and Rocky's charts. When he finished, he glanced at Inary who was doing her own charting.

"How do you like C2?" he asked.

"I've only worked here two days," she protested.

"Something tells me you're avoiding a straight answer."

She shot him an annoyed look. "I'm discovering it's not the same as working on a peds unit but I'm adjusting."

"Not ready to quit yet?"

"Why do people keep expecting me to quit? Actually, when I get used to these kids I might even enjoy working on C2." She turned to face him. "I was surprised to see you here on a Saturday evening—are you on call?"

He shook his head, offering her no clue as to why he'd visited the unit. "I seem to have arrived at the proper time, at least," he said.

"Yes, your being here saved me from having to notify the doctor on call. One thing puzzles me, though. Did you tell Mouse you were coming to see her tonight?"

"No."

"But she was at the door waiting for you."

"Mouse senses people she's attuned to."

She eyed him narrowly. "You told me once Enkidu was attuned to you. Are you suggesting Mouse is no more intelligent than a cat?"

"Don't denigrate the mind of a cat. Cats can sense things beyond human ability. But I had no intention of comparing Mouse to Enkidu." He rose. "Let's check on Rocky one last time and then you can see me out the door."

Rocky slept soundly. "He always does after one of his bad attacks," Mary reported. "He's going to be cross tomorrow, though. He always is the next day."

At the unit door, Ford said in a low tone, "I don't like to discuss anything of importance in public. If people overhear, they invariably misunderstand. We'll talk about Mouse another time. In private."

"I understand." She spoke stiffly, sounding, Ford thought, like a reprimanded child.

She couldn't know how difficult it was for him to maintain distance between them, or how hard it was for him to keep from touching her. Hell, she didn't even realize that the sole reason he'd driven to the hospital tonight was to see her.

"Good night." He reached for the knob.

"Ford?" she said softly, touching his sleeve.

He turned, gazing into her amber eyes, aching with his need for her. His "Yes?" was clipped.

She smiled tentatively. "Thanks for being here tonight."

Despite all his resolutions, he could no more resist her than he could resist breathing. He yanked open the door, pulling her through it with him, jamming his foot in to keep the door ajar. As he'd anticipated, at this hour there was no one in the outside corridor. He wrapped his arms around her and put all the longing he'd been repressing for the past two days into his kiss....

A few moments later, back on the C2 side of the door, Inary stood without moving, dazed.

I only wanted to share with him the good feeling I had about us working together professionally, she told herself. I didn't mean anything more.

At the same time, she couldn't help but wonder if she hadn't meant to prod him into exactly what had happened. Into kissing her. Because, deep down inside, she'd needed that kiss as much as he had.

CHAPTER SEVEN

Three days passed without Inary catching so much as a glimpse of Ford. She tried to convince herself it was just as well, but for some reason she missed seeing him. On Thursday morning, the cats woke her, as usual, earlier than she preferred. She stumbled downstairs, yawning, and let them out the shed door, gazing at a beautiful morning.

A perfect day to visit Agate Point.

Inary blinked, wondering where that thought had come from since Agate Point was the last place she wanted to go. On the other hand, if a patient forms an abscess, incision and drainage is usually the quickest route to healing. Maybe she needed to visit the point to begin her own healing. Why let one unpleasant incident from the past not only ruin her enjoyable memories of agate hunting on the point but keep her away from a part of her own property?

As she washed and dressed, her conviction that she must go to Agate Point as soon as possible grew, until she found herself rushing through breakfast.

This is ridiculous, she thought. Here, on the first of my two days off, I should be relaxing but instead I'm not even allowing myself a second cup of coffee.

The cats, as if infected by her urgency, ate very little of their own breakfasts. As she rinsed her dishes in the sink, the cats twined in and out and around her ankles, slowing her, forcing her to be careful lest she trip on them.

"What's the matter with you guys?" she demanded.

In answer, Gilgamesh flicked his tail irritably, a sure sign of annoyance. Enkidu favored her with an enigmatic yellow stare, as though turning the question back on her.

There was nothing the matter with her. Absolutely nothing. Having decided it was time to make a trip to the point, she merely wanted to do it stat. Quickly.

Though not quite T-shirt weather, the morning was the warmest since she'd come to live here. The April breeze, soft and southern for a welcome change, hinted of spring, and the bursting buds on the branches showed tinges of green.

Inary made her way to the crumbling old railroad bridge that crossed the stream and climbed onto the pilings with the cats following her. She trod cautiously on the few remaining rotting ties. When she came to the plank Ford had laid across a five-tie gap, Gilgamesh shot ahead of her, running over the plank, leaping from tie to tie on the other side and then jumping down into the underbrush and vanishing.

"Show-off," she muttered, eyeing the narrow plank with misgivings before stepping onto it gingerly.

When she was safely across, she looked back and saw Enkidu retreating rather than coming after her. Shrugging, she went on. There was no sign of Gilgamesh along the path between the birch and maple saplings, nor did she see him under the small stand of tall pines on the point itself. She went on, unworried, certain the cat could find his way back with no trouble. Though there was sand near the pines, the point's beach, several feet below where she had stopped, was pebbled with small stones.

Inary slid down the incline to the rocky beach, wondering what to expect. Would she be visited by ghosts of the past that forced her to relive what she'd tried so hard to forget?

She marveled that such a seemingly trivial experience could have had such a lasting effect, embedding itself in her mind with hurtful hooks of memory. Nothing so terrible had actually happened to her—she hadn't been raped, she'd only been humiliated.

Sighing, she crouched down to search for agates among the myriad of small stones washed by the gentle lap of the lake. But a strange restlessness gripped her, forcing her to abandon the search and hurry along the beach until she rounded the point and reached its western side, which was sandier, with fewer pebbles.

And a trespasser.

Even with his back to her, it was obvious he wasn't Ford, but a stranger. For a moment she was torn between prudently easing back to the other side of the point or more aggressively informing him that this was private property. Her property. Before she reached a decision, he turned.

Inary sucked in her breath.

"Fancy meeting you here," Roy Nuhaim said, smiling.

He expected me! The thought flashed across her mind as he approached.

Roy was even more handsome than she recalled, lean and pantherlike in black jeans and a black jersey. Why did she feel a strong urge to step back when he neared her? Holding her ground, she forced a smile.

"This is quite a surprise," she said coolly.

"Not at all," he told her, holding out his hand.

Though she raised her eyebrows at his comment, she felt obliged to shake his hand rather than behaving like a boor. After all, they weren't strangers. When he touched her, she regretted her action and would have withdrawn her hand immediately if she could have. But she found she couldn't move as repulsion warred with an odious excitement—she loathed his touch while at the same time she wanted to prolong the moment as long as possible.

The dart of anger that pricked her when she noticed a glint of triumph in his blue eyes was enough to give her the strength to pull her hand free.

"I've been looking forward to the day you'd return to Norwich," he said. "I've never forgotten you. How could I?"

Inary could think of no possible answer. She wanted to turn and run. She wanted to stay, to have him touch her again, to feel the excitement of—

No!

Looking away from him with an effort, she stared at the glitter of sunlight on the lake until her eyes watered from the glare, making her squint.

"We need time to become reacquainted," he said, his voice slithering silkily into her ears. "Are you free for dinner tonight?"

Not tonight. Not any night. Never. And yet she wanted to accept. Needed to accept. Afraid to open her mouth because she wasn't entirely certain whether she might agree or refuse, Inary swallowed. Twisting her hands together, she took a deep breath and let it out slowly. Why did he exert such a two-way pull on her emotions?

"You can't be afraid of me, Inary." He sounded amused. "Not when we've known each other for so long."

And so well, he implied.

His fingers briefly stroked the back of her hand and, to her horror, a thrill of anticipation shot through her.

"Do look at me, Inary," he said softly.

Reluctantly, she turned toward him, avoiding his eyes.

"Dinner tonight?" he repeated.

She had to give some sort of reply, but she feared what she might say. "I—" Inary began, pausing when she glimpsed something gray bounding from the trees.

"Cat got your tongue?" Roy asked.

Gilgamesh dashed down the slope onto the beach, stopping abruptly when he came between them. Fur raised, ears laid back, he spat as he glared up at Roy.

"Did you say something about a cat?" Inary asked, feeling, with relief, as though she'd been released from some kind of compulsion. Crouching, she crooned to Gilgamesh, who quieted and allowed himself to be lifted into her arms. But he kept a wary eye on Roy, the tip of his tail twitching.

Roy shrugged. "I take it yours is a one-woman cat."

Holding Gilgamesh made her confident, so she rose and faced him. "I believe so, yes. About dinner—I'll have to say no because I've made other plans."

He nodded. "My loss. But we'll be seeing one another again, I'm sure." Though he spoke lightly, she fancied she heard a threat in his words.

"I'm working at Sweetgrass so I *am* rather busy."

"Who isn't these days? Still, we can always make time for what's important. And we will." He smiled and, without a word of farewell, turned and walked away along the beach, heading west.

Not waiting to see him out of sight, Inary set the cat down, scrambled up the incline and hurried toward the railroad bridge. Fleeing, she admitted to herself. Why? Actually Roy had said and done nothing to frighten her, yet the entire time he was with her on the point she'd had a nagging sensation of something being askew.

Power attracts power. Ford's words. Was it possible—? She shook her head. How could she have any kind of hidden power without knowing it? As for Roy—Inary bit her lip, uncertain what it was about him that set her teeth on edge and yet drew her to him against her will. Power?

She crossed the makeshift bridge with Gilgamesh at her heels. Enkidu appeared before she reached the house, coming from the direction of Ford's.

"He's not home, he's working," she told the cat. Had Enkidu been aware Roy was at the point and tried to summon Ford to her assistance? Again she shook her head, wondering where these weird thoughts were coming from.

Be slow to dismiss what you don't understand. Neither ignorance nor obstinate blindness affords protection against peril. Aunt Inary's words, said to her— when? And why? She let herself and the cats into the house, still struggling in vain to recall what event in the past had led her aunt to warn her in this way.

Once inside the house, Inary rewarmed the coffee. Then, instead of pouring coffee into her own daisy mug, she lifted her aunt's green one from the hook and filled it. She sat at the table, cradling the green mug in her hands while she imagined herself as a child in this same kitchen, watching Aunt Inary drink coffee from the mug she was holding now.

She tried to picture her aunt at the table but another image formed instead: *Her aunt inside the room in the attic, sitting cross-legged on the red rug, a black candle burning to either side of her and a book open in her lap. Little Inary stood just inside the open door, smelling the candles' spicy scent and staring at the words on the pages of the book. She was old enough to read, old enough to know books were printed, not handwritten like the tattered old one her aunt held.*

Fascinated, she took a step into the room, drawn to the book, wanting to touch it, to read what she could of the spidery writing on its pages. She wanted the book to be hers. And then... then her aunt had lifted one of the candles and spoken to her....

The image disappeared.

Inary blinked, readjusting to the present. She took a sip of coffee, relieved that she hadn't slipped into one of her spells while recalling the vivid scene from her past. She clearly remembered that time, remembered the candles' smell and how much she'd wanted the book. But she recalled nothing more. Quite likely because there'd been no more.

At that point her aunt must have hypnotized her into forgetting not only the room but what she'd seen inside it. She'd recalled the room when Ford forced her to realize such a room existed, and at the same time she'd remembered the candles and the book. Not until this moment, though, had she known the book was handwritten and that the child she'd been had coveted it.

Where was the book now?

A sudden urgency gripped her, a need to find her aunt's book—the book she'd inherited. *Her* book. She set down the green mug and rose from the table.

After ransacking the upstairs and downstairs without success, Inary climbed into the attic and looked around at the barren room. Nothing here. Ford had told her that he cleaned out the attic at her aunt's request—but had it really been at her request? Could Ford's word be trusted? Had he found the book and kept it?

Her gaze fell on the cats, both standing between her and the locked room, staring at the door and then at her.

"Don't worry, guys," she said. "I learned my—" Inary paused. Hadn't she seen a chest inside that room? She was sure she had. Furthermore, Ford had mentioned something about black candles being inside the chest even though he claimed he'd never opened it.

If Aunt Inary's candles were in the chest, wouldn't the book be there, as well?

To find out if she was right she'd have to unlock the room and go inside. Recalling what had happened to her when she'd ventured in before, Inary shuddered. It wouldn't be a wise move. And yet if she didn't make the effort, she'd never know whether the book was in that chest or not.

I want that book, she thought. I *need* it.

What for? the rational part of her mind argued.

She didn't know the reason, but it didn't matter. She had to find the book. Without delay. Taking a deep breath, Inary made up her mind.

Trailed by the cats, she hurried down to the fireplace, opened her aunt's hidey-hole and retrieved the key. Back in the attic, she marched firmly to the door, unlocked it and flung it open.

Sunlight streaming in through the torn black blind made the room seem more ordinary. Nevertheless, she skirted the red rug rather than stepping on it as she crossed to the chest. The hidden pentacle might be more innocuous than Ford believed, but considering that her aunt had forced her to forget this room existed, she didn't care to expose herself to any more risks than she had already.

The cats, she noted as she dropped to her knees beside the wooden chest, were still with her, though their hair bristled. Holding her breath, Inary lifted the lid of the chest. The same spicy scent she recalled from her previous visits to the room drifted up to meet her, and she realized the odor must come from the candles.

She saw the candles first, wrapped in tissue paper as black as they were. Beside them lay a bundle wrapped in crimson silk. Inary picked it up, knowing even before folding back the silk cloth that she held her aunt's book. But the daggerlike knife she found with the book was a total surprise. When she gingerly touched its silver hilt, a strange tingling trickled through her. She jerked back her hand and quickly rewrapped both knife and book.

Dropping the lid of the chest into place, she rose and hurried from the room, carrying the wrapped bundle. Then she relocked the door and returned the key to its hiding place. Sitting in the rocker by the unlit hearth, Inary carefully removed the silk and gazed in satisfaction at the ancient book bound in cracked and flaking leather. Rewrapping the knife without touching it again, she set it aside and opened the book. Near the bottom of the first yellowed page, she recognized the sprawling loops and curlicues of her aunt's writing.

"Grimoire of Inary Morag Cameron," she read. Above this were seven other names, some repeating the Morag or the Cameron, but all repeating the Inary. Her name. She swallowed, a frisson of anticipation mixed with fear running along her spine.

Hesitantly, almost reverently, she turned the first page.

"Gather the petals when the moon is full," she read with difficulty, because the ink had faded and some of the letters in the handwriting were different from modern letters. "The roses must be white unless the pink wild rose is used. Only a virgin may pick the flowers...."

Inary paused and sighed, remembering her aunt gathering the petals with her in the moonlight.

Opening the book at random to another page, she found it written in another language. When she recognized *Unguentum* and *Quantum sufficiat* from her pharmacology classes, she realized the language was Latin.

"Protection," she read on the next page, which was written in a hand other than her aunt's. "The mountain ash or rowan tree is a safeguard against night wanderers, the red berries being especially potent in warding off evil."

Below this, Aunt Inary had added, "Fine specimen of rowan tree next to my house to right of front door. Am using its dried berries under the eaves."

Inary closed her eyes, remembering her aunt on a tall ladder poking red berries under the eaves. The child she'd been had had no idea why. The rowan still stood, straight and tall—she could almost reach out and touch its bare branches from her bedroom windows.

Opening her eyes, she saw, "To protect against binding invocations, agates must be collected on odd days of the month. Place three stones in each corner of the house while intoning a protection spell. Bury nine agates at the front and back entrances, again repeating the spell. Only those to be protected may gather the stones."

Inary recalled her aunt saying, "Well, child, how many pretty rocks did you bring me from the beach today? Ah, this white one will do. See how the wavy lines show up in the light? And here we have a brown one. White or brown, agates always have such lines. You've found two. Very good."

Protection, Inary thought. My aunt had me gather agates for my own protection. Before she died, she told Ford he must keep the house ready as a sanctuary for me, but long before that she'd tried to protect me with rowan berries and rose sachets and agates. Why did I need protection then? And why do I now?

Inary thought of the eight names written in the book and wondered if she was supposed to place her name under her aunt's, becoming the ninth Inary in succession to own the grimoire. And what exactly *was* a grimoire?

Her aunt's big old dictionary, kept on its own special stand in the living room, told her: "Book of witchcraft, magician's manual for invoking demons and raising the dead."

While she hadn't accepted the idea she might be a witch, it now seemed evident to Inary that her aunt had not only believed *she* was one but was convinced that her niece had inherited the talent.

Or curse. Inary shivered, gazing askance at the grimoire that she'd left on the seat of the rocker. Surely she'd know if she had any witch powers. Wouldn't she?

She'd never felt anything unusual about herself and she didn't now. Except for her spells—and how could they be considered power? Far from it! Because of the many quacks who'd tried in diverse and often odd ways to cure those spells, she'd once decided that every third person in California either believed or pretended to believe he or she had special powers, whereas, in reality, there were no such powers. Or so she believed at the time.

But then she'd met the night caller. Attracted him, according to Ford, because of her aura of unused power. She'd escaped the caller only because she'd fled thousands of miles to the safety her aunt had prepared for her.

Inary glanced around the familiar room. She did feel safe inside her house. Was it because of the rowan berries under the eaves and the agates buried in front of the doors and hidden in the corners? Did the scent of roses ward off evil? Maybe. But what waited for her outside? She couldn't and wouldn't stay shut up in here.

She watched in some surprise as Gilgamesh leaped onto the rocker and curled up on the open grimoire. You may not care for this book, he seemed to be telling her, but it suits me just fine.

Trust your cats, Ford had said. Could she? Inary wished she knew who or what to trust.

What she did know was she'd had enough of the grimoire for the time being. As though he sensed her intention, Gilgamesh jumped off the rocker when she approached. Deciding it was best to keep the book out of sight, she slipped it behind other books on the built-in corner shelves at the end of the living room and hid the silk-wrapped knife with it.

Noting that both the cats had stationed themselves by the front door, Inary lifted her denim jacket from the intricately carved coat rack in the entry and went outside with them. She'd dismissed Roy Nuhaim with enough finality that she was almost certain he'd be nowhere around, but still she lingered by the rowan tree, feeling oddly protected as she stood under its budding branches.

Gilgamesh soon returned, Enkidu trailing him, and climbed the tree, venturing onto a limb over Inary's head. With some effort, Enkidu managed to reach the same broad branch, where he crouched, looking pleased with himself.

As well he might, she thought. She'd never expected him to adjust so readily to the loss of his paw. Watching the cats, she noticed them tense, both gazing toward the drive. She turned to look, but there was no car or person in sight. Moments later, hearing a car engine, she grew as apprehensive as the cats. Since any mail was left in the two boxes by the main road, no one turned down the private drive unless they were coming here.

It wasn't quite noon. Ford was working today, so he wouldn't return from Sweetgrass until five or later, and she knew of no one who'd have any reason to visit her.

Inary drew herself up, suddenly angry at her paranoid behavior. Why should she be afraid? She was still chiding herself when Enkidu climbed down the tree and stood next to her, waiting. Almost immediately, Ford's car appeared in the drive.

Already surprised because he'd returned so early, she was even more startled when she saw him drive straight on to her place instead of turning toward his own house.

"I didn't expect to see you," she told him as he walked toward her after parking the car beside the tree. "You're home early, aren't you?"

Ford stopped to pick up Enkidu, who was weaving around his ankles. "Everything all right?" he asked, ignoring her question as he joined her under the rowan.

"Why, yes." It wasn't exactly a lie.

He stroked the cat's long dark fur for a moment before asking, "Then why are you standing here?"

Inary shrugged, reluctant to confess she felt safer under the tree. "No reason."

"I haven't had lunch. Have you?"

"No."

Ford smiled wryly. "Must I invite you to my house for lunch?"

Flustered—had her sense of hospitality deserted her entirely?—Inary said, "I'd be delighted to have you join me for lunch."

"I thought you'd never ask."

As they walked together to the door, she reviewed the contents of her refrigerator and frowned. Leftover guacamole dip, made the day before. A few spinach leaves. And four eggs. She had no bread left, only tortilla chips, and she'd scraped the bottom of the mayo jar to make the dip. She'd planned to shop for groceries this afternoon.

She'd have to mix the guacamole with chopped hard-boiled eggs, hope for the best, and serve the combination atop the spinach with chips on the side. "The special for lunch today," she announced with more confidence than she felt, "is egg salad, California-style."

Without being asked, Ford made coffee while she put the eggs on to boil. For some reason, this no longer bothered her the way it had when she'd first met him. In fact, she appreciated his help.

Carrying his mug of coffee to the kitchen table, he sat on one of the benches. Enkidu jumped up to join him.

"He's adopted you, I guess," she said.

"Not exactly." Ford absently stroked the cat as he spoke. "Enkidu and I have an understanding, but he'll never leave you to live with me."

She poured coffee into her daisy mug, bringing it to the table where she sat across from Ford. Gilgamesh settled at her feet. Since Ford didn't seem inclined to speak, Inary said, "I take it you're using more of your comp time."

He shook his head. "I'm working. I have to go back to the hospital after we eat."

She thought—but didn't say—that it was a long drive merely to eat lunch.

"What happened to you this morning?" he asked abruptly.

Inary stared at him. "This morning?"

"Stop echoing! Tell me."

"I walked to Agate Point," she said curtly, resenting his probing.

He nodded. "And something happened there. Something that frightened you."

"It's really none of your business," she snapped.

Gilgamesh removed himself from his spot by her feet and jumped onto Ford's bench next to Enkidu where all three—cats and man—seemed to glare at her.

"It's my business when you're so upset I can sense it from miles away," Ford said. "As I did this morning. Why else do you think I'm here?"

"What do you mean you sensed it?" Inary demanded, confused by what he'd said.

Ford took a deep breath, obviously controlling his temper. "I made the mistake of kissing you in my kitchen, if you recall. And you made the mistake of responding. Since we both have power, the physical expression of the attraction between us turned out to be enough of a connection to link us permanently. We are now bound to one another in much the same way Enkidu and I and Gilgamesh and you are attuned. I don't have to be with you to know when you're threatened. I sensed you were in danger this morning, but I couldn't leave the hospital to come to you until now. What happened?"

Inary pondered his explanation, not liking what she'd heard. Mistake? It certainly was! But not in the way he meant. She wasn't bound to anyone. Well, maybe to Gilgamesh, but certainly not to Ford.

"I don't believe I care to continue this discussion," she said, rising.

Ford sprang to his feet, dislodging both cats. They fled to the doorway into the dining room while he stood over her, glowering. "Do you think this is some sort of game?" he demanded. "I don't play games, either as a psychiatrist or a witch. Or as a man. If I say there's danger, I mean there's danger. Damn it, woman, do you want to be a victim? Who was on Agate Point with you? Was it the man you mentioned from your past—Nuhaim?''

She nodded. ''Nothing really happened,'' she muttered sullenly, still annoyed at Ford.

He closed his eyes briefly. ''I was afraid Nuhaim would surface sooner or later. It's obvious he has some sort of hold over you. I wish I knew exactly how strong that hold is.''

Inary exploded. ''I'm sick and tired of this talk of holds and bonds and attunements. I'm not attached to any man! Why can't you just leave me alone? You and Roy Nuhaim both.'' She banged her fist on the table, jarring her coffee mug and making the coffee slosh over the rim. ''I belong only to myself!''

He caught her clenched hand in his. ''For the moment, maybe. But you must know that both Nuhaim and I want you. One of us will eventually win, and when that happens there'll be no way for you to escape the consequences.''

CHAPTER EIGHT

Tasty as the avocado-egg mix turned out to be, the salad wasn't enough to overcome the antagonism flaring between Ford and Inary. The most tempting food in creation wouldn't have been enough to make the lunch a success, she told herself as she watched him leave for the hospital, knowing very well he was still incensed with her.

Not that she cared. Had she asked him to become her keeper? Begged him to save her from Roy Nuhaim? Insisted he be at her beck and call? No, no and no.

Never mind his talk of being attuned to any threat to her—she hadn't asked him to protect her and she didn't expect him to. Besides, she hadn't been threatened.

And about him claiming it was a mistake to kiss her—she certainly hadn't invited that kiss. About all she did agree with him on was that it had been a clear mistake for her to respond to his kiss.

"I don't know what you find to like about the man," she muttered at Enkidu as she washed the dishes. "He's the most arrogant, infuriating, annoying, interfering person I've ever met. And then there's all this nonsense about witches...."

Inary sighed, shaking her head. Much as she wanted to go on calling it nonsense, she no longer could. Not since she'd found the grimoire and understood that her aunt truly did believe in witchcraft and actually thought she could perform it. Aunt Inary, in her own mind at least, had been a witch. And the seven other Inarys before her had obviously shared this strange belief.

To be fair, I should give Ford the benefit of the doubt, she told herself, and accept the fact that he, too, believes he's a witch.

Was it possible she herself might have unexplored powers she'd never tried to discover? Inary half smiled. If so, any such powers were well hidden. Wait, though—at the California hospital where she'd worked as a nurse, hadn't she had some success in helping a few of her patients with the laying on of hands? She'd always felt their improvement might be due to the power of suggestion rather than any innate power she possessed, but what if she was wrong? What if her success was due to something within her?

She really would like to possess the power to heal, to help the sick and infirm. She wouldn't even mind being labeled a witch if she had such an ability. Was there any chance she did have a reservoir of untapped healing power? Still, even if she did, how could she learn to use it to help others?

Ford could teach me. The thought came unbidden, and though she tried to reject it, she could not. Finally she nodded reluctantly. Even if he couldn't help her, Ford was the only person she knew who wouldn't laugh at such a request. She'd have to swallow her pride and talk to him about it.

Inary had no chance that evening, because Ford still hadn't returned home by the time she went to bed at eleven-thirty. She half roused around one, thinking she'd heard his car, then fell asleep once more. He'd left for work before she got up on Friday morning.

This was the day, she remembered, that she'd promised to join Wheatie and two other Sweetgrass nurses for a fish-fry supper at Spurwood Lodge. At six-thirty. Quite likely she wouldn't have time to see Ford before she left for the restaurant.

It was a sullen April morning, spitting a thin, cold rain at intervals, not the kind of day she enjoyed being outdoors. The cats agreed with her, seldom asking to be let out and then spending only the necessary few minutes before dashing back into the house again.

Inary spent the day catching up on put-off housework, doing a washing and reviewing her nursing textbooks for tips on caring for mentally handicapped children. She found a few helpful suggestions but nothing that seemed to apply to Mouse.

In the late afternoon the rain ceased and the clouds parted to reveal such a spectacular red sunset that Inary dallied on the beach to see its full glory, making her late for her six-thirty meeting with Wheatie and the others.

Knowing Yoopers—as some of the younger people in the U.P., or Upper Peninsula, had begun to call themselves—tended toward casual dress, she hurriedly donned a denim jumpsuit and short boots, putting on her denim jacket as she stood in the open doorway trying to coax the cats inside before leaving.

Both Gilgamesh and Enkidu refused to obey her, so at last she reluctantly locked the door and got into her car, unhappy to leave them out after dark. She reassured herself as best she could with the thought that she'd certainly be home well before midnight.

Ford's car, she noted as she pulled away, wasn't parked by his house, so he hadn't gotten back yet. Perhaps he planned another late night. Whatever he did was none of her business, but she couldn't help wondering where he'd been last night until after midnight. With a woman?

Surprised and upset by the undeniable twinge of jealousy she felt, Inary quickly and firmly thrust him from her mind.

She found Spurwood Lodge without difficulty, a large barnlike building a few miles outside of Norwich, set off the road amidst pines and spruces. It was almost seven when she left her car in the dimly lit parking lot.

When she stepped inside the lodge, the smell of fish and hot fat surrounded her, the strong odors all but obliterating the smell of stale beer. Like many such places in the U.P., Spurwood was obviously a bar first and a restaurant second. Cigarette smoke drifted overhead and cold swirled around her ankles as Inary searched the crowded room for Wheatie, noting that every available booth seemed to be taken.

Finally, way in the back, she saw a wildly waving hand and spotted Wheatie's blond hair. Wheatie came to meet her before she reached the booth.

"Sorry I'm late," Inary said.

"Laine and I were late, too," Wheatie confessed as she led Inary toward the back. "Mostly because we stopped for Kelly. She'd met some new guy and he asked her out so she changed her mind about coming with us but she forgot to let us know. Anyway, everything was jam-packed by the time we got here. But, hey, luck struck. This guy Laine knows—he's a real hunk, wait'll you see him—was sitting alone and he invited us to join him.''

From what she'd been told, Inary had expected Laine, the day charge on C1, to be sitting with the man she knew, but as they neared the booth, she saw Laine was alone. The man, his back to Inary, was sitting opposite Laine.

"I found Inary," Wheatie announced when they reached the others. She slid in next to Laine and gestured at Inary to sit opposite them. "You get the seat of honor, okay?"

After greeting Laine, Inary turned to smile politely at the man. She froze.

"Hello, Inary," Roy said. "Better late than never."

Aware both the other women were watching her, Inary forced herself to sit down beside Roy. "I didn't expect to see you," she told him, keeping her voice deliberately light.

"You two know each other?" Wheatie asked.

Inary nodded.

"We told you her name and you never said a word," Wheatie accused Roy.

"He's a man of secrets," Laine said.

Roy smiled. "Like all attorneys. Actually, Inary and I have been friends since we were children." He put his hand over hers as he spoke.

She drew her hand away. He'd certainly stretched the truth but she didn't feel inclined to try to explain how it had really been. They might have known each other in the past but they'd never been friends. She glanced at him and saw his gaze fixed on her, his blue eyes glittering like the lake on a cloudless day.

Inary had the strange sensation time had stopped for her alone, leaving her in an isolated pocket of silence while noise eddied about her, unheard. A pulse throbbed in her neck. She turned away from Roy and focused her attention on Wheatie, who was talking, and sound broke through the barrier, but Wheatie's voice blended with the background bar babble and her words made no sense. Inary gritted her teeth and concentrated.

"... all by herself out there," Wheatie finished.

When all three of them looked at her, Inary realized Wheatie must have been telling Laine and Roy—he already knew—that she lived alone by the lake.

"Isn't it rather lonesome?" Roy's words slid into her ear.

"I do have one neighbor," she said.

"Yeah," Laine put in, "I heard you live almost next door to Dr. Werlich."

"Werlich," Roy repeated. "Do you know him well, Inary?"

"We've met." She lifted the glass sitting in front of her, a drink she didn't recall ordering, and took a sip. It proved to be a screwdriver—her choice on the rare occasions when she decided to have a drink—but it was so strong she almost choked.

Since there was no straw or stirrer in the glass, she poked at the ice cubes with her finger, hoping to dilute the vodka.

"Did you know Dr. Werlich's supposed to have killed a patient where he worked before he came to Sweetgrass?" Laine asked.

"I've heard the rumor." Inary spoke more tersely than she'd meant to. She wasn't defending Ford, not exactly, but since he apparently had never been arrested or even lost his license, maybe it *was* only a rumor.

"I don't know him well," Wheatie said, "but I think a lot of shrinks are sort of weird, you know?"

A man and woman stopped at the booth, greeted Wheatie and Laine and began talking to them. When Roy leaned closer to Inary, she sipped nervously at her still-too-strong drink, wishing she hadn't come.

"It seems we're having dinner together, after all," he murmured. His words were soft, his voice warm, but when she glanced at him she noticed his eyes were as icy as the waters of Lake Superior in winter.

"I always get what I want," he added, running his fingers along her arm to her hand. Lifting her hand, he eased it onto the seat between them and covered it with his own.

Though he held no more than her hand, she had a strange sensation of being trapped, caught in some kind of invisible web, unable to find a way out. She wanted to free her hand but somehow could not. Looking away from Roy, she fought to regain control of her will, her gaze drifting unseeingly over the many faces in the room, until suddenly her vision cleared and she found herself staring at Ford Werlich, who was leaning against the bar.

He scowled at her. Annoyance burned through her. Did Ford think she was with Roy by choice? And, even if she had been, what business was it of his who she was with? Damn it, she belonged to neither of them!

She turned away, jerked her hand from under Roy's, grabbed her glass and took two hefty swallows of the screwdriver.

"Your friend Werlich apparently doesn't approve of us being together," Roy said, his voice pitched so low only she could hear.

"He's not my friend," she snapped before she thought, then wished she'd ignored the comment.

Though she really didn't like the taste, unease made her continue to sip at her drink until the glass was empty. Head spinning, unhappy at being here with Roy, she desperately wanted to get up, march out of Spurwood and go home to her cats.

But then Ford might think she'd left because of his disapproval, which certainly was *not* the case. Besides, that overly strong screwdriver on an empty stomach had left her a bit muzzy—in no condition to drive. She'd have to wait and hope that eating would clear her head. How long would it be before anyone came to take their order?

The drink must have been a double—something she'd never order. Who *had* ordered it? Roy? Was he trying to get her drunk? For some reason that struck her as funny and, to her horror, she heard herself giggle.

A waitress passed, carrying a tray of food, and the odor of fried fish wafting Inary's way brought a wave of nausea. Oh, great, she thought. That's all I need.

"I think I'll get some fresh air," she muttered, rising and easing into her jacket.

"I'll go with you." Roy slid from the booth before she could protest and took her arm.

Feeling too ill to argue, she allowed him to guide her to the door. Once outside, she took deep breaths of the clear, cold night air and her nausea began to ebb.

"Feeling better?" he asked after a time.

She definitely was but she couldn't yet face going back inside Spurwood and inhaling those pungent odors. "Maybe a little," she temporized, wishing her thoughts weren't so fuzzy.

"Let's go for a drive." His arm around her shoulders, Roy started to lead her away from the building, but when they reached the parking lot she halted abruptly and jerked free.

"No, thank you. I don't want to." Not with Roy. If only her head would clear, she'd drive herself away from here. Away from him.

"We'll walk then." Taking her hand, he pulled her along with him to the far end of the lot where the dim lights didn't penetrate.

Not a good idea. She was about to say so when he backed her against a black car—his?—and put his arms around her, under her jacket. His lips covered hers, warm—too warm, unpleasantly warm. She didn't want—didn't like—his kiss, and yet at the same time she felt an unwelcome trickle of response run through her. She had the confused impression she was reliving a dream.

No, she thought. No. But she couldn't move. Once again her will wasn't hers to command. In some frightening, incomprehensible way, he controlled her.

Roy's kiss deepened, his tongue forcing its way between her lips, invading her mouth, a violation she was helpless to prevent. She resented what he was doing, and yet, in some hideous, perverse way, she wanted him to go on.

Hating what was happening to her but unable to resist, Inary began to cry.

He laughed. "You're mine," he murmured into her ear. "You can't help yourself."

"Nuhaim." The voice came out of the darkness. Ford's voice, grating across her taut nerves.

Roy released her and spun around. She straightened, trembling, holding onto the car for support. The two men stood facing one another, dark silhouettes in the uncertain light.

"She hasn't chosen you," Ford said.

"She has no other choice," Roy countered.

"There's always a choice."

Roy didn't reply. Though neither man moved, Inary sensed power crackling between them and had the distinct impression that, in some esoteric way she didn't comprehend, they were dueling.

She was startled when an owl hooted four times from the pines crowding close to the parking lot, its mournful cries loud in the quiet night. Somewhere in the distance a dog howled. Was it a dog? Inary shivered, but the two men ignored the sounds.

The door to the lodge opened. Music and voices and laughter spilled into the darkness, seeming to shatter the stasis gripping Ford and Roy. Without so much as a backward glance at her, Roy skirted around Ford and sauntered toward the lodge, behaving as though he'd merely taken a turn in the fresh air. She watched him vanish inside before turning to Ford.

It was too dark to see the expression on his face, but she could imagine his shuttered, cold look. Disapproving. Shutting her out. "Give me the keys to your car," he said, his voice betraying no emotion.

Though she desperately wanted to go home and knew she was still in no condition to drive herself there, she bristled. "Why?" she demanded.

"The keys," he repeated.

Light-headed, her stomach still on the queasy side, she stopped resisting, dug into her bag and slapped the keys into his hand.

"Can you walk by yourself to the car?" he asked.

"Certainly!"

Once fastened into the passenger side, she laid her head against the seat back and closed her eyes. She wasn't aware of drifting off, but when Ford stopped the car she came to herself with a jolt, uncertain where she was.

As if aware of her confusion, he said, "We're home."

Her house key was on the ring with her car keys. Ford unlocked and opened her front door, letting the waiting cats enter first. Then he ushered her inside, dropped the keys on the small table in the entry and walked past her to the kitchen. She heard him running water in the sink.

Who'd asked him in? Annoyed, she marched into the kitchen. "What do you think you're doing?" she demanded.

"Making coffee."

"I don't recall asking you to. I can take care of myself."

"Can you?" He went on measuring coffee, without so much as glancing at her. "You certainly fooled me."

"I didn't order that damned double screwdriver!" she snapped, then could have bitten her tongue. No matter who'd ordered it, no one had forced her to drink the screwdriver, as he was certainly aware.

He didn't bother to comment.

Inary slumped onto a bench, put her elbows on the table and propped her chin in her hands. The cats jumped up to either side, nestling close to her. They offered comfort but she needed more than that at the moment. "I don't feel good," she said mournfully.

Ford set her daisy mug in front of her and put the black-and-white one on the table for himself. "Your own fault," he said.

It was. She couldn't deny that.

While the coffee dripped, he made toast, buttered it and set it along with a jar of peanut butter, on the table. Then he poured the coffee and sat down. Slapping peanut butter on a slice of toast, he handed it to her and ordered, "Eat. And drink your coffee."

"I don't—"

"You'll keep the toast down and then you'll feel better."

He was right. After finishing two slices of toast and two cups of coffee, she felt almost herself again.

"I'm not much of a drinker," she admitted. "Alcohol tends to make me sick."

He nodded. "That's why I came after you. Choice is one thing, coercion another. If you, in full possession of your faculties, decide to jump in the sack with Roy, I won't like it but I won't try to stop you. Tonight you might not have been staggering drunk but you obviously weren't clearheaded. So I interfered."

"But why do you care?"

He sighed. "Let me go over it once more, as bluntly as possible. One, you have power. Two, you don't know how to use that power. Three, so far you've refused to try to accept or to learn more about what you are. Four, you're still a virgin, so your dormant power is vulnerable. Five, others with power, like the night caller and Nuhaim, have tried and will keep trying to steal your power for themselves by being the first to bed you."

She gaped at him, speechless. Could she believe everything he'd just told her? And how the hell did he know she was a virgin?

"I think Nuhaim has some hold over you," Ford added, his gaze intent. "Am I right?"

Remembering how she loathed Roy's touch yet had also been unwillingly attracted to him, Inary swallowed her pride. "I—I don't know. I think he might."

"Your aunt told me about finding Nuhaim trying to seduce you on the point when you were fifteen."

Her face flamed. Why on earth had her aunt revealed such a humiliating episode to Ford?

He reached across and took her hand. "She was afraid for you, fearing that if you returned to the Upper Peninsula, Nuhaim would go after you again. That's why she told me. What did you give him when you were fifteen?"

She took a deep breath, hating that Ford knew about her teenage escapade but ready to admit she needed help where Roy was concerned. "The only thing I ever gave him was an agate I found on the point."

Ford winced, gripping her hand tighter. "That's worse than I thought. Agates protect. In giving him one you found, you gave away your protection." He reached for her other hand, holding both. "If he's kept that agate, and I fear he was aware enough even then to have held on to it, we're in real trouble."

The *we* warmed her as much as the comforting grip of his hands. Ford was on her side. He meant to help her. "What can I do?" she asked.

"As a starter, stay away from Nuhaim if possible. Accept no invitations from him."

"I'll stay away." Belatedly recalling how difficult it was to say no to Roy in person, she amended her words. "I'll try to, anyway."

"Remember, this house is safe. At least, so far."

"I'm beginning to feel nothing else is safe. I went to Spurwood Lodge tonight to join some of the nurses from work. And look what happened. I admit some of it was my fault but I didn't expect Roy to be there, I really didn't. How could I?"

"Expect him to turn up often," Ford said grimly, releasing her hands. "Anywhere and everywhere."

"Not at the hospital, surely."

"Probably not there, but don't count on it. Don't count on anything where's he's concerned. Nuhaim's a real danger to you, Inary. Other than trying to avoid him, what do you intend to do about it?"

"What can I do? I found my aunt's grimoire, but—" She broke off, realizing she hadn't intended to tell him.

He was silent for a time, finally saying, "The grimoire must have been in the chest. That means you went into the locked room alone again."

"Nothing happened this time. I didn't even have a spell."

"A vision."

She ignored his correction. "I found the book and came right out. Since you tore the blind down so the sun can shine in, the room doesn't seem so sinister."

He got up and drew her to her feet. "Believe me, it is. You were lucky to get out unscathed. You might not be so lucky the next time. Promise me you won't unlock that door again without telling me beforehand."

"Well, I—"

He took her right hand and placed her palm over his heart. "Promise."

Enthralled by the intimacy of the gesture and by an intangible bond that suddenly seemed to connect them, she whispered, "I promise."

He was close to her, so close she could feel the warmth of his body. Looking up at him, she found her own desire reflected in his expression. But he made no move. She knew he wanted to kiss her—why didn't he?

She slid her hand up from his chest and touched his lips with her fingers, watching his eyes begin to smolder, heated by desire.

"You're damned difficult to resist," he murmured, pulling her into his arms.

Ford's kiss was everything she wanted and more. Yet at the same time, his kisses, no matter how wonderful, were not enough to satisfy the hunger he awoke within her. When his lips trailed down to her throat, she threaded her fingers through his hair, whispering his name as a plea for him to go on, to take them both farther, take them all the way, take them to a place she'd never been.

Still holding her close, his lips at her ear, he whispered. "I want you so very much. Not for power but for yourself."

"Yes," she murmured. "Oh, yes."

He grasped her shoulders and held her away from him. "No," he countered, his voice hoarse. "Oh, no. Our making love might solve your problem with Nuhaim, but if you lose your virginity before you use your ability you'll be crippled without a chance to know what you could be. I can't do that to you, Inary."

"How noble of you," she said coldly, hurt by what she saw as his rejection. She tried to free herself from his grasp, but he wouldn't let her go.

"Damn it," he growled, shaking her. "I've never wanted a woman so much in my life as I want you. Not only now. Continually. Ever since I first laid eyes on you. But even if it kills me, I'm going to allow you the time to discover what you are."

"What if I don't want to be a witch?" she muttered.

"You *are* one, even though your power's still untapped. Since you were able to find the grimoire without harm, your aunt must be looking after you. To do that, what remains of her has had to stay behind instead of going on. That's a tremendous sacrifice to make. If you won't do it for yourself, or for me, learn for her sake, Inary. So her spirit can rest in peace."

CHAPTER NINE

Inary awoke the next morning with a headache and with the gloomy feeling she'd handled the events of the previous evening very poorly, first with Roy, then with Ford.

It would *not* be a good idea to see Roy again, she told herself, unable to understand how she could have allowed him to manipulate her the way he had. From now on she'd do her best to avoid him completely and hope she never had to deal with him again.

Ford was another matter entirely. Since they were neighbors and also worked at the same hospital, she couldn't very well avoid Ford. And admit it, she didn't want to avoid him. They'd arranged that on her way to work this afternoon she'd drop him off at Spurwood to retrieve his car. Though she half dreaded seeing him, she also looked forward to it.

Then there was the witch business. As she ate breakfast, Inary brooded over what Ford had told her the night before and came to the conclusion that if she made a concentrated effort to study her aunt's grimoire, maybe she'd begin to understand the power Ford claimed to have. And said *she* had.

Despite her fuzzy-headedness in the parking lot the night before, she couldn't deny Ford had bested Roy without a word and without laying a finger on him. Through some strange power?

Power or not, it had humiliated her to need rescuing, and she was determined never to put herself in such an embarrassing and potentially disastrous situation again.

She spent the rest of the morning poring over the grimoire, learning that the silver-handled dagger she'd found wrapped in silk with the grimoire was called an athame, otherwise known as a witch-knife.

This athame was very old, handed down like the grimoire from the first Inary, and the crescent designs of inlaid ebony on the hilt represented the moon, the source of power.

"The athame," her aunt had written, "must never be used as an ordinary dagger—to kill by penetration—lest it be so badly contaminated it can never be renewed by the moon's rays. Proper use of the flat of the blade will banish evil. Each new adept in the line must consecrate the athame anew and bind it to herself by believing with her heart and soul in what she does as she performs the moon-binding ritual."

"*I* am the new adept," Inary said aloud, not quite able to believe her own words, much less believe in the moon-binding ritual.

Yet even while doubting she'd ever find the belief necessary to make the athame hers, she recalled the inexplicable tingling current that had shaken her when she first touched the witch-knife and felt certain it *was* more than an ordinary dagger.

At the moment, wrapped in silk, the athame lay where she'd hidden it, beneath the blankets in the cedar chest at the foot of her bed. There, Inary thought, the witch knife would probably remain.

Ford arrived just before two. Facing him proved not to be as difficult as she feared, partly because he didn't refer in any way to what had happened at Spurwood Lodge.

"You don't have to shut the cats inside when you leave today—or any day that you work," he told her. "I'll keep an eye on them. Lock the house but leave the shed door unbolted, and I'll make sure to put them in the shed when it gets dark. Okay?"

Inary agreed, pleased with the idea. As the weather grew milder, both Gilgamesh and Enkidu enjoyed being outdoors more than in. This way, she could be certain they were safe inside the shed after dark and could let them into the house proper when she got home.

"Have you gotten better acquainted with Mouse?" he asked as she drove him toward Spurwood.

"I think so. I don't quite understand how, but we seem to communicate even though she doesn't speak or make signs to me."

He nodded. "I hoped she'd realize what you were. Once you gain full use of your power, I'd like to try working with you to see if we can't help Mouse. She's got untapped potential."

Inary half smiled. "Like you claim I have."

"In a way. Except that Mouse will never be a witch. Still, with our help, she ought to improve enough to become a relatively normal child."

"That would be wonderful, if it's possible. But why can't you do it alone?"

"One isn't enough. It takes two with power, sharing their power. I learned that at a terrible expense."

Inary glanced at him and saw he was staring straight ahead, his face set and grim. He turned to her and added, "I need help. Your help."

She recalled the rumors she'd heard about Ford causing a patient's death downstate. Were they true? Had he tried to use his powers on a patient and had the experiment ended in disaster?

"I wouldn't want Mouse hurt in any way," she said apprehensively.

"Nor would I. Whether you believe me or not, I've learned my limitations. Perhaps you'll come to trust me one day."

Would she? He claimed the California night caller had wanted to use her power and he insisted Roy was after the same thing. She didn't disbelieve him. But was Ford being completely honest in saying he needed her power only to help him with Mouse? Did he want nothing for himself? There was more to this than he was saying, she was sure.

And why were the night caller, Roy and Ford so positive she had hidden power when she wasn't at all certain she actually did? She thought of the grimoire with its list of Inarys and nodded. Maybe the power existed, but she certainly didn't have a clue how to evoke it. Unless the athame—?

"Do you have a witch-knife?" she asked abruptly.

He shook his head. "Mine is earth-power, not moon-power like your aunt's. Like yours. Since you've brought up the subject, I take it you found her athame with the grimoire."

"Yes, but—" She shook her head.

"Make the athame yours as soon as you can. Before the end of the month."

She frowned. "The end of April?" Even as she spoke, she remembered him saying the thirtieth was Walpurgis Night, when dark power is strongest.

"I don't know if I can," she told him. Or if I really want to, she added silently as she swung into Spurwood's parking lot and pulled in beside his car. The sight of the lodge made her grit her teeth as she recalled last night's humiliation. Still, she owed him.

When Ford reached for the door, she touched his shoulder and he turned to her. "I'm not proud of the way I behaved last night," she admitted. "Thanks for your help."

He smiled, lifted her hand from his shoulder and brought her palm to his lips before opening the door and sliding out. With a nod of farewell, he closed the door and turned away.

As she watched him get into his car, Inary found to her dismay that she was pressing her hand to her own lips as though to transfer the kiss. Shaking her head at such foolish romanticism, she turned the car around and left Spurwood Lodge.

Wheatie had today off, sparing Inary from having to make explanations about Friday night. She'd face that problem tomorrow, when Wheatie returned to work. After Inary finished the busiest part of the shift—the first three hours—she found that the nurse assistants assumed she wanted to be the one to put Mouse to bed.

"You can't deny that little girl's taken to you," Erma Beech said. "Why, she watches every move you make. Been good for her, too. When you're on duty she don't sit in a corner with her hair over her face."

"She's a sweet little thing," Inary said.

Erma exchanged a significant glance with Diane, who worked when Mary had an evening off. "I guess maybe you do mean to stay on, at that," Erma said to Inary.

Erma must believe my interest in Mouse is a sign I can accept these children, Inary told herself, realizing that the assumption was true. Not merely because Mouse intrigued her but because, after a week of being with them, she'd come to think of all the C2 patients as "hers."

When she offered Mouse her hand, ready to lead the little girl to her room, Mouse tugged her in the opposite direction and she followed the child, finding herself in Sunny's room. Mouse pulled her to the railed bed where Sunny, the biter, lay restrained.

As she looked down at Sunny's twisted face, a picture formed in Inary's mind of a chaotic, confused, churning roil of fragmented images. She felt a terrified anger and knew it came from Sunny. Without thinking about what she meant to do, she released Mouse's hand, pushed the head of the bed away from the wall and stood behind it to place her left hand on Sunny's forehead, then her right hand atop her left.

She closed her eyes, the better to clear her mind, and began visualizing calmness—the peaceful waters of the lake in the blue twilight, the moon floating serenely in a sea of stars, herself sitting quietly in the rocker stroking a purring cat. This world was not chaotic but ordered. The sun came up every morning to warm and light the earth. Pines rose in stately forests. Rivers ran, wide and dark and deep, to the lake, whose waters washed constantly back and forth on sandy and rocky beaches alike....

After a time, Inary's eyes opened. Without removing her hands, she glanced at Sunny, who seemed to have fallen into a peaceful sleep. She took her hands away and eased herself out from behind the bed.

When she looked at Mouse, she saw the child was smiling.

Driving home after work, she mulled over the incident. Inary thought that her laying on of hands had offered temporary relief to Sunny and hoped she'd be able to help in this way again. But how had Mouse known Sunny's need? For there was little doubt Mouse had deliberately led her to Sunny's room because she wanted Inary to help the other little girl.

Even more disturbing was that Mouse had somehow been able to show her Sunny's disordered, angry, frightened mind. How?

Mouse realizes what you are. Ford's words.

What was she? And, what, for that matter, was Mouse?

She arrived home with no satisfactory answers to any of the questions she'd asked herself. Finding the cats in the shed, as Ford had promised, she let them into the kitchen and they trailed her up to bed.

Waking to a cold and rainy morning, Inary lit a fire in the fireplace after breakfast, planning to sit in the rocker while she studied the grimoire for possible answers to the questions that plagued her.

She had no more than settled herself comfortably, the cats at her feet, when the phone rang. She picked it up on the fifth ring.

"Are you still speaking to me?" Roy asked.

"I answered the phone." She spoke coldly. He had his nerve!

"You have a right to be upset about Friday night," he said smoothly. "I realize I came on too strong. My only excuse is that you do something strange to me, Inary. I don't seem to be able to think clearly when I'm with you. And, of course, I didn't know you had a thing going with Werlich."

"Actually, I don't. But I certainly agree that you behaved badly."

"Werlich seemed to feel the two of you had an understanding. I'm happy to hear he's wrong. I do hope you'll find it in your heart to forgive me for losing my head over you."

Though her memories of the evening were somewhat fuzzy, she recalled enough to be unwilling to accept his apology and to become angry at him all over again. "It really doesn't matter whether I forgive you or not," she said with finality, "because I won't be seeing you again. Goodbye, Roy." She hung up before he had a chance to respond.

So much for Roy Nuhaim, she thought as she settled back into the rocker. Still, she wished he didn't live so close. Ironwood couldn't quite be called a neighboring city, but it was only seventy miles away.

She'd been as blunt as possible in discouraging Roy, but just as a precaution, maybe she should have let him go on believing there *was* an understanding between herself and Ford. Opening the grimoire again, she pushed Roy from her thoughts.

"I bought the house because of the pentacle," Aunt Inary wrote, "never realizing what a burden I'd be taking on. Though those with powers beyond my own assure that the five-pointed star within the circle can be used for good, as I hoped to use it, I fear the one in my attic room has been so imbued with evil before my ownership that no spell or charm can ever cleanse this pentacle again.

"Worse, I find myself tempted against my will to call up abominable forces by using this evil star. Fortunately I've proved strong enough to resist. Another problem has been seekers-of-the-dark, drawn to the power of the pentacle. Over the years, many, under false pretenses, have attempted to beguile me into inviting them into my house, but I'm quite clever at seeing through masks and have discouraged them all.

"After I was forced to send my young niece away, I vowed that as long as I live no one will enter the pentacle room, not even myself. The exception will be when I place this book in the chest with my athame, knowing I'm leaving the house and will never return again.

"Except for the one room, my house is a haven, a place of safety for the child when she needs it. True, when I die, she will inherit the problem of the pentacle, but that cannot be avoided. I have made certain she doesn't know the room exists. Against the day she discovers it, I shall set down what she must know."

Inary's head was whirling by the time she finished the list of precautions. Once inside the circle of the pentacle, she learned, provided the proper spell had been used, nothing from the outside, not even an evil force, could pass the barrier of the circle, so the one inside the circle was safe from harm. Only the use of a fully powered athame could break the circle.

Other preventive powers of the athame were mentioned, but she barely skimmed them. As she understood it, she couldn't use the athame until she was bound to the knife, and she wasn't at all certain that would ever be possible because she lacked the necessary belief.

Later, at the hospital, Inary found Wheatie needed no explanation about Friday night.

"I'm sorry you weren't feeling well," Wheatie said. "Roy told us how Dr. Werlich met the two of you in the parking lot and offered to drive you home." She leaned closer. "I think Laine was secretly pleased because then Roy took *her* home—she's got a real thing for him. Did you get along with the doctor okay?"

Inary nodded.

Wheatie lowered her voice. "Is he as weird as they say?"

Inary avoided the question entirely by saying, "I was sick, remember?"

"Well, anyway, I'm sure Laine figures you did her a favor."

If it means Roy is now interested in someone else, Inary thought, perhaps Laine did *me* a favor, as well.

The evening was quiet and so were the rest of the evenings she worked that week. By the end of her shift on Wednesday, though, she was ready for her two days off.

Either by accident or by design, she hadn't seen Ford since she dropped him off at Spurwood the previous Saturday. Though she was honest enough to admit she missed him, she was determined not to make the first move.

When the cats woke her on Thursday morning, the first of her days off, Inary was delighted to see sunshine. As she came down the stairs, she was surprised to see the cats heading for the front door rather than the back, their customary preference.

"Anything to be different," she muttered to them, before noticing the folded paper on the entry floor, a paper that had obviously been thrust under the door.

She picked it up to read while the cats complained about her delay in opening the door.

"'Beach bonfire tonight at dusk,'" she read, after some difficulty in deciphering the writing. "'Hot dogs, marshmallows, the works. You, me and the cats.'" F.W. was scrawled underneath.

I might have known Ford wrote it, she thought with amusement as she let the cats out. Doctors in general wrote so illegibly that it was a standing joke among the nurses who were forced to read their scribbles that med schools must offer special courses in bad penmanship.

Underneath the amusement, she bubbled with an eager anticipation she tried to quell by telling herself that he took a lot for granted. What if she'd already made other plans? It would serve him right if she stuck a note under *his* door saying she couldn't make the beach party but the cats would be delighted to join him.

Unfortunately, so would she.

After breakfast, both she and the cats were enticed outside by the warm sun and the mild breeze. With spring finally making tentative but unmistakable advances, it was no time to sit in the house reading ancient tomes.

"Listen," she told the cats as they followed the path to the beach. "I hear swamp peepers. That's a sure sign of spring."

When she returned from a long walk up the beach, she was overjoyed to spot the green thrust of her aunt's crocuses in a sunny bed near the house. They weren't yet ready to flower and, crouching beside them, she tried to recall what colors they were. White, yes, and purple and lavender. Yellow? She wasn't sure.

One year, she remembered, deer had come and eaten every last flower. "I must plant more daffodils" was all her aunt had said. "That's the only flower they won't touch." Inary hadn't seen any deer since her return, but they must still be around.

She stood, raising her arms above her head in a salute to spring's arrival, and took a deep breath of pine-scented air. This was meant to be her home. It *was* her home. She belonged here. No one and nothing would or could drive her away.

To her surprise, because he so rarely wrote, the mail brought a letter from her father. Before the end of April he'd be off to South America again to build a bridge in Peru.

"I hope you'll be all right living alone by the lake," he wrote near the end of the letter. "There's something about that house of my sister's I never liked."

She sat holding his letter, warmed by the unusual, if slight, evidence of his affection. He'd never been a demonstrative man, and Inary had often felt she was no more than a burden to him. His comment about the house startled her. Though he'd referred to it as a white elephant, her father had never before mentioned any dislike of the house. Nor had he, in general, ever shown any evidence of being sensitive to atmosphere.

It seemed strange her unimaginative father had felt an aversion to the house, whereas she, who was supposed to possess power, felt nothing of the sort. The cats, too, had taken to the house. Except, of course, for their fear of the locked attic room. But she doubted that her father knew such a room existed.

Did he realize his sister had been a witch, that the Cameron genes apparently passed the trait along to female children? Certainly he'd never mentioned this, nor would he, Inary was sure, be able to accept it as a possibility. Even if they'd been closer, she wouldn't be able to confide in her father and expect him to believe her problems were real.

Toward evening, she changed from jeans into a warm turquoise jogging suit. Though the day had been balmy for an Upper Peninsula April, the air would grow chilly once the sun set. By the time she was ready to go to the beach, the cats were waiting impatiently by the back door.

"How come you guys always seem to know what's up?" she asked. In answer, Gilgamesh gave her his imperious feline stare that hinted at secrets cats shared with no one.

Inary smelled wood smoke when she stepped outside, telling her Ford had the fire going. The cats bounded beachward ahead of her in the fading light, Enkidu not quite able to keep up with Gilgamesh. They reached the driftwood fire before she did and, when she arrived, were perched on a large log conveniently near the flames, watching with interest as Ford unpacked the food basket.

"I hope you don't object to them eating junk food on special occasions," he said as she came up.

"What, and spoil their fun?" she asked. "They'd never forgive me."

He grinned at her, looking as relaxed as she'd ever seen him in a blue sweatshirt and jeans. Relaxed and enjoying himself. She smiled back at him, feeling a sudden spurt of pure happiness. Happy because it was a glorious evening, made beautiful by the calm and silvery lake to one side and the dark rise of the pines to the other, because nothing threatened her or her cats on this peaceful beach, but mostly because she and Ford were together.

"Hungry?" he asked, his gaze holding hers.

She nodded, not looking away, not wanting to look away from the glow in his dark eyes. Was it only the reflection of the flames or an inner gleam that matched her own insistent flicker of desire?

The fire snapped, shooting out a spark that flared as brightly between them as the rising tension. If she didn't say something, if she didn't move right now, this minute, she'd have no control over what might happen.

"I had a letter from my father," she said with effort, easing down onto the log beside the cats. "He mentioned that there was something about my house that he never liked. It surprised me."

"What was it he didn't like?"

Inary shrugged. "He didn't say. I don't think he knows. I don't feel the same way—not at all."

"I do."

She gaped at him, astonished.

"The first time I entered your aunt's house," he said, "I had to conquer a deep-seated uneasiness. I'm still not entirely comfortable in the house, even though I've found the reason—the pentacle in the attic room. I knew the room was there but I didn't realize the pentacle existed until you found the key."

"I don't like the idea of the pentacle being there," she said slowly, "but I can't say it really bothers me. I'm perfectly comfortable living in my house and so are the cats."

He nodded, glancing at the cats. "They sense your ease."

Enkidu jumped off the log and trotted over to Ford, raising himself on his hind legs to peer into the food basket.

"If you insist," Ford told him, removing two hot dogs from a package. Taking a knife, he sliced them into two small aluminum pans, then offered one pan to Enkidu and the other to Gilgamesh.

"The soft drinks are in the cooler," he told Inary. "Help yourself."

"I'm not as impatient as the cats," she said, looking up at the darkening sky where stars were beginning to pop into view. There was no sign of the moon.

"Full moon at the end of the month," he said, as though following her thoughts. "On Walpurgis Night."

The binding spell for the athame called for a full moon, she recalled, but she was sure she wouldn't be ready to try by then. Maybe she would never be.

Ford handed her a long wooden-handled fork with a hot dog impaled on each of its two prongs.

"We're supposed to wait until the fire dies down into coals," she protested.

"You claim you're not impatient, but admit it, did you ever actually wait that long?"

She laughed as she eased the fork into the fire. "Never. You've discovered my secret. Is discovering secrets a talent you learned in your psych residency?"

"No such luck. My fame, such as it is, rests on good guesses." He thrust his fork into the flames. "This takes me back to my childhood and summers at my grandparents' cottage on a small lake in Vermont."

"You're a New Englander?"

"They were. I grew up in Ohio."

She'd opened her mouth to ask him more about his past when he pointed to her fork, warning, "Watch out."

Seeing her sizzling hot dogs were close to total incineration, she pulled her fork back and tried to find a spot where they'd cook without being burned to a crisp. She wasn't quite successful, but knew that even charred hot dogs could taste good when the setting and the company were perfect.

Later, sitting next to Ford on a blanket, their backs propped against Gilgamesh's log, Inary sighed as she watched her marshmallow turn golden brown in the heat from the coals. "Why can't life always be like this?" she asked.

"I suppose because we're human."

She frowned at him. "Don't turn into a shrink before my very eyes."

He smiled and said, "Your marshmallow's done."

She pulled the toasted marshmallow gingerly off the fork and offered it to him.

"Ladies first," he said.

"Isn't that chauvinistic?"

"Not when I know perfectly well the first one to take a bite burns his mouth on the hot center."

"Chicken." Inary lifted the marshmallow to her lips and took a cautious nip. Hot, yes, but not burning. "Mmm," she said teasingly, biting off more.

Ford leaned to her, saying, "Now I'm ready to take a taste." As he plucked the remainder of the marshmallow from her lips with his own, he pulled her close.

Moments later they were stretched out on the blanket, wrapped in each other's arms. As he kissed her, under the sweetness of the marshmallow she tasted and savored his dark and exciting masculine flavor. His lips didn't insist—they promised, a promise she longed to have fulfilled.

Unlike when she'd been unwillingly embraced by Roy, she wasn't compelled by some strange power outside herself to respond. Her response rose from deep inside her, unmistakably her own desire.

She liked being exactly where she was. Except *liked* wasn't strong enough, it was more than a liking. Much, much more. With all her heart and soul, she felt she *belonged* in Ford's arms.

CHAPTER TEN

As he lay on the blanket under the stars with Inary in his arms, at first Ford was able to ignore everything but the ever-more-powerful urge to possess her. He was dimly aware of the soft lap of the waves, the occasional crackle of the coals and the courting songs of the spring peepers, fit background music for making love.

His fingers slid under her shirt and caressed her bare skin—how warm it was, how smooth. She tasted sweet—her scent, spice and woman, aroused him. She fit against him as though they'd been made to come together. Her eager response fired his blood. She was the most exciting, enticing woman he'd ever known.

Then there was the other, the tingle of power meeting power, making him anticipate a strange and wonderful completeness when they joined, unlike anything in his experience and beyond his imagination.

He wanted Inary as a woman, he desired her with a desperate yearning. But he couldn't deny the strong additional lure of her nascent power. The combination overwhelmed his remaining doubts.

Yes, his body, aroused almost beyond bearing, urged, yes, make love with her. Now.

As he undressed her, alternately touching and tasting her everywhere, her lips, her body, her moans of passion assured him she wanted what he wanted.

Tossing the last shreds of reason aside with his clothes, he started to rise over her.

Pain stabbed, sharp as needles, into his right calf, raking down to the ankle. He cried out in surprise and pain, twisting away from her, turning to see what had attacked him.

Side by side, the cats glared at him. Gilgamesh, fur raised, spat while Enkidu growled.

Furious, he raised his hand, then held, struggling with his anger. Damn the two of them, they were right. The cats had reminded him, in the only way possible to them, what he already knew. Never mind how much he wanted her nor how much she thought she wanted him—he was taking unfair advantage of her.

Inary rose on one elbow, staring from the cats to Ford's scratched and bleeding leg. Had they attacked him? "Ford?" she asked.

He got to his feet, his back to her. "Get dressed," he rasped.

Not understanding exactly what had happened, she found her clothes, and as she pulled them on, both cats joined her, one to each side. Like guardians, she thought, not altogether happily.

She watched Ford, now dressed, walk to the waterline and stand looking over the dark lake. Uncertain what to do or say, she remained where she was.

"Don't blame the cats," he said at last, turning and coming toward her. "I should have remembered they'd take care of you."

Take care of her? But she *wanted* Ford to make love to her. Why would they attack him?

"I thought," she said, smoothing her hair, "that Enkidu was supposed to be attuned to you."

"They're still your cats, not mine. Especially Gilgamesh. He led the attack."

"But he likes you."

Ford smiled wryly. "Only if I keep to my place in the scheme of things. He let me know I overstepped." He crouched and, holding out his hand, said to the cats, "No hard feelings."

Enkidu moved to rub against his knee, but Gilgamesh only deigned to sniff his fingers.

She glanced from Ford to the cats and back. "You mean they'd attack any man who tried to—I mean, well—"

He rose. "Make love to you? I don't know. Both of them are aware I'd never hurt them so they don't fear me. But if they were afraid—" he paused, shaking his head "—they might be too terrified to attack someone dangerous to them."

"I still don't understand why Gilgamesh scratched you."

"I've explained it before. You haven't yet gained the full use of your power, and until you do, I know better than to make love to you. The problem is, when you're close to me I keep forgetting."

He ran his fingers along her jawline to the hollow in her throat, where he could feel, she was certain, how even this light caress had sped her pulse.

"I guess the only solution," he said, "is to try to teach you. I've taken tomorrow off—we'll begin then, after breakfast at my house."

"But—"

He held up a hand. "I hope you like oatmeal."

She smiled tentatively. "Aunt Inary long ago convinced me I did."

"I imagine the cats will prefer to roam the woods, but if they want to come with you, they're welcome." His gaze held hers. "Do you want to learn?"

She took a deep breath before nodding.

"Good. Any questions?"

Inary hesitated, then decided she had to know. "One. Why are you so sure I'm a virgin?"

"I sense your power—you shine with it. But you don't use it. Before you came here, you weren't even aware you possessed power. In both men and women, witch power is tied in with virginity. In either, the power has to be known and used before the first sex, otherwise it's lost or flawed. Or controlled by someone unscrupulous enough to take advantage of an innocent."

Inary considered what he'd said. "What happens after the first sex if the person is already using the power?"

"Men usually continue to have power. Women, unfortunately, may lose theirs. I don't know why this is so."

The grimoire, she recalled, had mentioned something about only virgins being able to gather rose petals. "You mean I could gain use of my power only to lose it?"

"Yes. But at the same time, no one else could control you through the use of your own latent power."

"In other words, night callers and such will quit chasing me once I learn what to do with my power whether afterward I remain a virgin or not."

He grinned. "By George, you've got it!" Leaning to her, he kissed her forehead.

"I realize it's taken me a long time to believe you," she said. "I still find it hard to accept."

"But you do accept that you have power and you intend to learn how to use it."

Inary sighed. "I've run out of other choices."

When she arrived at Ford's the next morning, minus the cats, he smiled and said, "I see they've decided I've learned my lesson."

After breakfast, he led her into the living room where, in the fireplace, flames flickered low as the fire died away into coals. A black vase on an end table held seven large scarlet poppies, their brilliant color brighter than the fading flames. Hadn't some poet she'd read called poppies "hell flames"?

When she and Ford stood directly in front of the fire, he turned her to face him. "Have you ever heard of capnomancy?"

She shook her head.

"It has to do with flowers," he said. "You'll discover what it means as we go along. You begin by looking into my eyes."

"Don't try to hypnotize me," she warned.

"No, nothing like that."

She took a deep breath, telling herself she trusted him, and gazed into his dark eyes with their intriguing amber wedges.

"Don't think," he continued. "Choose a place inside your head and fix on it but don't close your eyes. Sometimes it helps to repeat a letter or a word over and over under your breath. The important thing is to trick your brain out of both beta and alpha patterns."

"Something like meditation."

"But not quite the same." He reached to the table, plucked one of the poppies from the vase and handed it to her.

"When your mind is quiet," he said softly, "look at the poppy instead of at me."

Inary was accustomed to closing her eyes when she cleared her mind for the laying on of hands, but she discovered that by focusing on one particular diamond-shaped amber spot in Ford's left eye, she could free her mind. As her surroundings gradually blurred, her thoughts trickled away and vanished.

Her gaze shifted to the black heart of the flower she held, darkness surrounded by hellfire. After a time, the petals of the poppy seemed to expand, ballooning until they enclosed her within the flower, within the scarlet flames. . . .

"Throw the poppy onto the coals and watch it burn." Ford's voice came faintly, as though from a distance.

Slowly, she leaned toward the grate and dropped the flower on top of the coals. Smoke rose, white and gray, as the fragile petals crumpled in the heat. Smoke rose, twisting from the dying poppy, and Inary saw Roy's face form in the swirls. Darkness gathered around his face, expanding until it encompassed and blotted out Roy, swelling from the fireplace into the room, reaching to engulf her.

She screamed, thrusting her hands in front of her to ward off the darkness. "Go back, go back!" she cried.

Suddenly there was no darkness, nothing but a fireplace with a charred poppy disintegrating to ash on the coals.

"What did you see?" Ford asked.

She turned to him, aware now of her surroundings but still frightened and bemused. "You knew I'd see something," she accused.

"Not *know,* exactly. I expected you to, yes. But I have no idea what you saw in your vision. Tell me."

Vision. Inary shivered. That's what he called her spells. But this hadn't been a spell, this was different, she hadn't lost consciousness. She did her best to describe what she'd experienced with the poppy.

Ford pursed his mouth in a soundless whistle. "Nuhaim. I'd hoped he'd given up."

"Roy wasn't the darkness," she said. "Whatever that was, it swallowed him up before threatening me. I think I—" She hesitated. "Didn't I push the darkness away from me?"

"You called, 'Go back, go back!'"

Inary nodded. "Yes, I remember."

"So now we know Nuhaim's still a menace."

"Maybe so, but in my—my vision, the darkness was far more frightening."

"He may very well be connected with that darkness." His face set in the cold, hard planes she disliked, Ford yanked the other six poppies from the vase and flung them onto the embers.

She watched him stiffen as, hands at his sides, he gazed at the smoke rising and coiling while the flowers were consumed. Anguish distorted his face, then horror blanked it. She twisted her hands together apprehensively. What did he see?

At last he turned from the fireplace, and she reached for his hand. "Ford?" she said softly.

He gripped her hand so hard she winced. "It's worse than I ever imagined," he said hoarsely. "Evil lies in wait. Darkness and evil. You're in deadly danger."

Inary bit her lip. "Danger from what?"

"Nuhaim's mixed in with it, he's the cause." Ford dropped her hand and rammed his fist into his own hand. "If only I'd seen more, seen enough to know how to keep you safe."

"I'm not going anywhere near Roy Nuhaim, you can be sure of that!"

He gazed at her bleakly. "But will that be enough? I doubt it. I've had a bad feeling about Walpurgis Night ever since you arrived. I greatly fear the evil we both saw just now is connected with that night. I wish I could keep you with me twenty-four hours a day, until after Walpurgis Night was history. And even then . . ." He shook his head.

Impressed by his obvious alarm, she asked uneasily, "What should I do? What *can* I do?"

"You've demonstrated your power with your vision when the poppy burned. Since you were able to thrust back the darkness you saw, you've learned to use some of that power. Read the grimoire. Learn as much as you can as fast as you can."

She swallowed. "I'll try."

"With April 30 less than two weeks away, trying isn't enough. Reach out with your power. Use your power."

"Can't you show me how like you did with the capnomancy?"

He took her hands in his. "Divining with flowers is easily demonstrated and easily learned. Though useful in its way, to those with power capnomancy is the equivalent of a parlor trick. I can't teach you what you really need to know to be strong enough to save yourself. The athame, for example—I have no moon—power, I can't help you bind the knife for your use alone.''

"There *is* a ritual with the moon," she admitted.

"A vital ritual, yes. But the belief in the athame must come from deep within you. Search for that belief, Inary. Search hard."

He dropped her hands, turned and walked away. She remained where she was, staring at the red eyes of the embers and wondering if the vibrant energy she felt coiling inside her had come from her use of power. Her power. She could hear her heart thudding in her ears, its beat sped up by excitement and apprehension. She really *did* have power like the other Inarys of her bloodline. She really *was* a witch. How wonderful! And how terrible.

She shook her head, asking herself what it actually meant. Would her life change abruptly? Not that she could see. She didn't intend to move from her house by the lake and obviously she must continue working, not only because she needed an income but because she valued helping others.

If there was danger ahead, as Ford insisted, maybe she'd be better fitted to face it now that she knew she had power to call on—if that power came when she called.

When she returned to work the following day, Inary was intercepted by Laine on C1 before she reached the door to C2.

"I'm sorry you got sick at Spurwood," Laine said. "I hope you're feeling okay now."

"I'm fine," Inary assured her.

"Good. I'm off this weekend and I was thinking maybe the two of us could have lunch together. Around here somewhere, 'cause I know you're working evenings both weekend days."

About to agree, Inary paused to think. Hadn't Wheatie mentioned that Laine was interested in Roy and that he'd taken Laine home that Friday night? Still, what harm could there be in joining Laine for lunch?

"I'd like to," she said.

"Great. There's a place on the highway to the left as you're coming into Sweetgrass. It's called Cousin Jack's and they make fantastic pasties. Say about one on Saturday?"

Inary went on to C2, wondering if Laine's invitation had been prompted by something other than friendliness, then chided herself for paranoid thinking.

The unit was quiet that evening except for Rocky having a grand mal seizure as he was being put to bed, but to Inary's relief, it didn't last abnormally long. When she went to collect Mouse from the dayroom, she found the child drawing with the colored markers and paper she'd brought as a present.

"May I see?" she asked, kneeling beside the little girl.

Mouse offered a sheet of paper.

Inary was taken aback to find Mouse had drawn a recognizable poppy with bright red petals and a dead black center. Coincidence? It must be. And yet, why did a black cloud hover over the flower?

She'd meant to praise the drawing, but instead half whispered, "How did you know?"

Mouse stood in front of the kneeling Inary and placed a hand on either side of Inary's head. A vision formed in Inary's mind—smoke rising as the poppy burned on the hot coals. She swallowed and took Mouse's hands into her own.

"Time to go to bed," she managed to say, for the moment unable to face any more strangeness. She remembered to add, "I'll help Sunny after I tuck you in."

Inary repeated her laying on of hands with Sunny and had the satisfaction of seeing the girl fall asleep without sedation. But as she left Sunny's room, the image of Mouse's poppy began to burn all over again in her mind.

Mouse's diagnosis was severe autism, but Inary no longer believed the girl was autistic. Nor did she believe Mouse belonged in a state hospital. Inary thought of what Ford had said about the two of them working together to help Mouse and she nodded. She wanted to and she would—as soon as she learned how to use her power in ways that could help.

The next afternoon at one, she found Laine waiting for her in a booth at Cousin Jack's.

"They sell beer here if you want one with your pasty," Laine said as they ordered.

"Even if I wasn't going to work, I rarely drink," Inary confessed. "Alcohol and I aren't terribly compatible. I'll have coffee."

After a brief flurry of hospital talk, Laine said, "I've always thought nurses ought to stick together, no matter what. We take enough crap at work, we don't deserve it on the outside."

Though not having the slightest idea what Laine was getting at, Inary nodded.

"So, anyhow," Laine went on, "I made up my mind to tell you what's going down. I mean, he's a dream come true and sexy as hell, but I don't like to be used. And I was. I am."

"He?" Inary ventured.

"Roy. I didn't realize what he was doing at first, not even when he so conveniently and supposedly by chance saved us a booth at Spurwood. I mean, he came on to me and so I thought he was interested—hoped he was, anyway. Even after he maneuvered things so you sat with him at Spurwood instead of me sitting with him, I didn't figure out what he really was after until two days ago. He's stalking you, that's what he's doing."

"Stalking me?" Because she had no intention of telling Laine any more than she had to, Inary tried to sound more surprised than she was.

Laine nodded. "I'm pretty sure his only interest in me was so he could find out what your days off were and anything I knew about what you might be doing, like going to that fish fry." She stared at Inary.

"I don't want anything to do with Roy Nuhaim." Inary spoke with the conviction she felt.

"Yeah, well, I figured that. But I thought you ought to know 'cause I don't think Roy's the type to give up easy-like." She sighed. "I wish he wasn't so damn hard to resist."

Knowing firsthand what she meant, and feeling sympathetic, Inary covered Laine's hand with her own for an instant. "Thanks for telling me. I'll be on guard."

Laine frowned, thought a bit and then nodded. "Yeah, those are the right words, after all. 'On guard.' They sounded weird when you said them—I mean, we're not talking serial killer or like that—but I have a gut feeling Roy means to get what he goes after and not necessarily by fair means, either. I wish to hell I'd never met him."

Inary silently echoed her wish.

As the days passed, she did remain on guard, but nothing frightening or unusual happened. And, though she studied the grimoire diligently, she found no clear instructions on how to free her power. Sometimes she sensed a coil of energy building in her, but nothing more. And though she saw Ford every day, at least briefly, he seemed to have distanced himself from her emotionally, making her feel deserted.

April 26, the last of her two days off for that week, dawned rainy and cold. Resigned to staying indoors, Inary sat herself in the rocker and opened the grimoire, the cats at her feet.

"Keep moonlight from the pentacle," she read, "lest you be tempted to use the power to call up evil." She started to turn the page, aware the pentacle wouldn't be of help to her, but then hesitated. The handwriting was her aunt's, and, curious to know more about how Aunt Inary had felt about the pentacle, she read on.

"The Book of Solomon tells us the most powerful of the dark forces can be evoked when the moon's rays fall on the pentacle at the same time the water beats on the shore. Keep, therefore, a black blind nailed to the window to prevent any gleam of moonlight from creeping into the room."

Ford ripped the blind down, Inary recalled, to let in daylight. He must not have known the danger. She ought to buy another black blind to replace the torn one.

"I wish I could forget that the pentacle exists," her aunt had continued. "The evil star calls me when I'm least equipped to resist. After I realized how dangerous the room was and kept it locked, vowing not to enter, I've found myself standing inside the circle three different times without remembering how I got there. Finally I made a new hiding place for the key and set a talisman to guard it. Since then, though I've been plagued with dreams of incubi, I've not gone near the pentacle.

"Rose sachets, as I've learned from reading those who have come before me, are effective in repelling incubi, though not their lustful mortal counterparts. Fortunately, I'm able to repel such mortals myself."

So the iron owl on the raised brick hearth is a talisman to guard the key, Inary thought. But were dreams of incubi the reason Aunt Inary always wore a rose sachet pinned to her nightgown?

It was difficult to believe everything she read in the grimoire. Nevertheless, she meant to replace the black blind as soon as possible. And maybe tucking a rose sachet in her pocket wouldn't hurt, either.

Somewhat to her surprise, Norwich's one cluttered hardware store proved to have a black blind in stock. "This blind ain't what you'd call new," the elderly clerk warned her, "so I can't guarantee how long it'll last. The way I figure, it's been around almost as long as I been working here."

Back at home, Inary removed the key from under the brick and, the cats trailing her, climbed the attic stairs. Because of the rain, the light in the attic was dim. With the cats watching, she unlocked the door and, carrying the blind, a hammer and nails, entered the locked room. It was gloomy in the gray light but not actually sinister.

Setting what she'd brought on the floor beside the chest, Inary turned to look at the rug. On impulse, she swept it aside to stare at the inlaid pentacle. A five-pointed star within a circle—why had it so tempted her aunt? It had no influence over her—none at all. She was in here merely to replace the blind.

Then why was she opening the chest instead of climbing on it to nail the new blind to the window? Why was she removing the three black candles? Where had the alien words circling in her mind come from?

And then she ceased to think....

"*Bagahi laca Bachabe,*" she murmured, feeling herself drifting into darkness.

She heard voices chanting—or was it one voice? Yes, a man's voice. He stood inside the pentacle, his back to her, intoning words she didn't know but yet, in some undefinable way, she understood. Three black candles burned within points of the star. The man raised his hands above his head and started to turn toward her.

A cat wailed. No—two cats, yowling in unison. Their piercing cries hurt her ears, distracting her so the man's face blurred and she could no longer follow his words. She must shut the door to mute the sound.

But the cats stood in the doorway, preventing her. The largest, gray and white, glared at her with brilliant green eyes. The smaller, long-haired, had but three paws....

Light seemed to flood her mind, banishing the man and his dark words. Enkidu. Gilgamesh. Her cats, both of them. Warning her, calling her to safety. To her horror, she saw she was lying inside the pentacle. Abandoning any notion of replacing the blind or retrieving the hammer and nails, she scrambled to her feet, fled through the door, slammed it shut, turned the key in the lock and then flung the key down the attic stairs for fear she'd be tempted to return to that terrible room.

I had another spell, she told herself, shivering. The worst I've ever had. I can't go on like this—who knows what might happen the next time?

In her bedroom she lifted her prescription bottle from her chest of drawers. Would it be dangerous if she doubled her dosage? She hesitated, unable to decide.

Ford would know.

But he was at work. Did she dare wait until he came home? She glanced at her watch to see how long that would be and drew in her breath. It was after three! Her spell had lasted more than fifteen minutes, longer than any other. She hugged herself, frightened and miserable. What should she do? Chance the wait? Or take a double dose and hope for the best?

She sat on the bed, the bottle in her hand, unable to make up her mind. The cats jumped up, crowding close to her, trying to climb into her lap. She knew they were trying to comfort her, but how could they when she felt beyond any comfort? Though she kept telling herself she had to get up, had to make some kind of decision, she didn't move.

Not until the front door slammed open downstairs. Inary leapt to her feet, startled.

"Inary!" Ford shouted. "Where are you?"

She had to clear her throat before she could speak. "In my room."

He pounded up the stairs and stopped short in the doorway of her bedroom. "Are you all right?" he demanded.

"No," she wailed.

He strode to the bed, pulled her to her feet and into his arms, holding her gently. Not caring how or why he was here, she leaned against him, sighing, desperately needing the strength that flowed from him.

After a time she pulled back and offered him the prescription bottle she still clutched in one hand.

He looked at the label, his eyebrows rising. "You're not taking this, are you?" he demanded.

She nodded.

"What the hell for?"

She took a deep breath, eased it out and began the long story of the strange spells that had started when she was between eleven and twelve, the many failed treatments, Dr. Janowicz's diagnosis and how the spells had gotten worse since she'd come here.

"I'm so afraid of becoming a vegetable," she finished, her voice breaking.

Glaring at her, Ford tossed the bottle onto the floor and, while she gaped at him, he stomped on it, crushing plastic and pills alike.

CHAPTER ELEVEN

"What have you done?" Inary cried, staring from Ford to the shattered plastic and the crumbled white pills on her bedroom floor. "That was my medicine."

"And damned dangerous," Ford snapped. "This particular drug should rarely be given, and then with extreme caution. Janowicz must be an idiot to have prescribed it for you."

"But it did work," she protested. "I didn't have those spells as often. Not until—"

"You didn't have spells, you never had spells. You had visions. A manifestation of your power that began with your menarche and has nothing to do with any kind of epilepsy, aberrant or otherwise."

"Then why did my electroencephalograms show abnormal brain waves?"

"Different, maybe, but not abnormal. Not for you. Do you think witches have the same EEG patterns as everyone else?"

Inary blinked. "I—I never thought about it. But still—"

"No more buts. You don't need any medication and especially not what you've been taking. He *did* have enough sense to keep the dosage minimal, so I don't think you'll develop any dangerous long-term effects." Ford glanced at her bed and shook his head.

"Let's continue this downstairs. I'm too easily tempted as it is."

Her mind in a whirl, Inary followed him into the kitchen, sitting on a bench as she watched him go through the familiar routine of making coffee.

"That seems to be *your* prescription for everything," she muttered.

He glanced at her. "What? Oh, coffee. Why not? It's certainly safer than what you were taking. Another thing—I thought I warned you to keep your doors locked at all times. The front door wasn't."

"I keep forgetting. My aunt never locked her doors, except at night."

"She didn't need to. You do."

Belatedly remembering how he'd slammed into the house, shouting for her, Inary said, "You scared the wits out of me coming in like you did."

"When I sensed you were in trouble, I broke every speed law in the book getting here from Sweetgrass. Did you expect me to knock?"

"Never mind. I'm glad you came." She waited until he'd poured the coffee, set the mugs on the table and eased onto the other bench before she told him about trying to replace the black blind in the locked room.

"When I came to, I thought I'd had one of my spells," she said as she finished, "but you claim it was a vision."

"Because it *was*. What you saw while you were lying in the pentacle either will happen in the future or has happened in the past."

She cradled the mug in her hands, feeling the hot coffee warm her palms and wishing she could as easily banish her inner chill. "Will I go on having these—these visions?"

He nodded. "Eventually, when you gain control, the visions won't be so random—you'll be able to choose when to have them."

"I hope you're right."

"I am." He scowled. "Fugue state. Of all the nonsensical prognoses he could have come up with, that's the most ridiculous. I've a mind to call Janowicz and—"

"He's out of the country until June," she told him with relief. If Ford was right, and she prayed he was, Dr. Janowicz had certainly been wrong, but he *had* tried to help her.

"Is there anything else you haven't seen fit to share with me?" he asked.

Inary shook her head. She hadn't shared Laine's warning about Roy but she saw no point in doing so since both she and Ford already knew Roy was best avoided.

"Until you control your power," he said, "you should encourage these visions. They may help you learn."

Encourage them? She winced inwardly. Didn't he understand how she hated what happened to her? Up until this moment she'd taken everything Ford had said on trust. But could she—should she—trust him completely?

"I know it's early," he said, "but I missed lunch. Come on, we'll go somewhere and grab a bite to eat."

Inary glanced at her jeans and faded T-shirt with its dancing raisins logo. "Like this? No way."

He shrugged. "So we'll get take-out pizza or something and bring it to my house."

"I've got some homemade spaghetti sauce in the freezer," she said. "I can thaw it out and cook the pasta to go with it in less time than it would take to drive into Norwich, and bring the stuff back."

"You've sold me. Let's take the sauce to my place and we'll cook there."

She started to argue, then recalled his confession that he, like her father, wasn't quite comfortable in this house. "Fine."

Working beside Ford in his kitchen, with the wail of Boots Randolph's yakety sax in the background and the cats underfoot, Inary smiled. The first time she'd set eyes on Ford Werlich, she'd labeled him cold, distant and arrogant—the last man she'd ever expected would fit into a cozy, domestic partnership such as they shared at this moment. And he was also the last man in the world she could have imagined falling in love with.

Startled by this last thought, she stared blankly at the strands of pasta clinging to the fork she'd just lifted from the steaming kettle. In love? With Ford? Was she out of her mind?

"Not too al dente," he said. "I'm a sort-of-mushy type."

It took her a moment to realize he was referring to the pasta. She nodded absently and returned to arguing with herself. Okay, so she wanted Ford in a way she'd never experienced with any other man. But that alone wasn't love. She enjoyed being with him, she trusted him as much as she trusted anyone, and when they were together she felt safe, she felt secure. And happy.

But—love?

Later, after they'd eaten and were relaxing in the living room in front of the fire, with Gilgamesh purring beside her, she watched Ford stroking Enkidu, who was curled in his lap.

"Domestic, isn't it?" he said.

Almost the same thing she'd told herself earlier. "I wish—" she began, then hesitated, reluctant to reveal herself by what she'd intended to say. *I wish it could always be this way.*

He looked at her expectantly. She was searching for less revealing words when Gilgamesh suddenly sat up, ears perked as though listening. Enkidu stayed on Ford's lap, but his eyes were open and alert.

What had spooked them? Usually, she'd found, whatever they'd sensed brought no danger to either her or the cats. Still, it always unsettled her.

"Cats so often seem to hear things humans miss," she said, eager to change the subject. "That's not so bad, but it really unnerves me when they seem to *see* what's invisible to human eyes."

"They make very good guardians. Actually better than dogs in some ways, though dogs do make superior attackers."

"Are you thinking of getting a dog?"

He shook his head. "The most vicious of dogs wouldn't be of any use to either of us. Dogs have no defense against the forces of the dark. Cats, on the other hand, often survive."

Feeling herself tense at his words, she sighed inwardly, telling herself, So much for domesticity.

The phone rang and Ford deposited Enkidu on the floor as he rose to answer it. Listening to his end of the conversation, Inary realized he was talking to someone at the hospital and that he must be on call.

"I really must run along," she said when he hung up.

"Your spaghetti sauce was the best I've tasted," he told her. "Thanks for having supper with me."

Though his words didn't lack sincerity, she thought he spoke as though his mind was elsewhere. "Do you have to go to the hospital?" she asked.

"I'm not sure yet. I'm the administrative doctor on call and I'm hoping what I suggested to the medical call doctor will solve the problem. But—" he shrugged "—I'll wait and see."

He walked with her to the door and, before opening it, leaned to her and kissed her lightly, his lips lingering on hers, the kiss beginning to deepen when the phone rang again.

"Goodbye," she said hastily and left.

They'd eaten early; it wasn't dark yet. As she and the cats walked toward her house, Inary gazed at the sunset-reddened clouds, telling herself that if sailors knew what they were talking about with their "red sky at night," tomorrow should be a delightful day.

Instead of running ahead of her as they usually did, the cats crowded close to her feet, but Inary paid little attention, her mind on the kiss at the door and what might have happened if the phone hadn't rung the second time. She'd almost reached her front door when she thought she heard Ford start his car. Apparently he did have to go to the hospital, after all.

Since he'd insisted she lock her doors, Inary had her key ready as she started up the steps to the porch.

"Inary." The voice came from behind her. She froze, recognizing the man's voice.

With an effort, she turned and saw Roy skirting her car as he approached the porch.

"I didn't mean to startle you," he said.

"Then why were you hiding behind my car?" She glanced around. "And where is *your* car?"

"I walked."

She raised her eyebrows. "From Ironwood?"

He smiled disarmingly. "No, along the beach from the cabin I'm renting near Norwich."

"And just what are you doing here? I thought I made it clear I didn't care to see you again."

"Abundantly clear, alas. Never have I goofed quite so badly as I did with you. I wish you could find it in your heart to forgive me."

As he spoke he eased toward her, and she found herself retreating onto the porch where both cats huddled against the front door.

"Actually," Roy went on, climbing the steps, "I wanted to show you something." He reached inside his jacket and pulled out a crystal pendant hanging from his neck on a thin gold chain.

"I don't want to see it," she said coldly. "I don't care to have anything more to do with you. Now, if you'll excuse me—"

"Just one quick glance." He dangled the crystal before her eyes so that she couldn't avoid looking. She saw there was an agate set within the crystal and then found that she couldn't tear her gaze away from the agate, no matter how hard she tried. Roy's voice dropped to a whisper:

"You gave the stone, you gave your will

"To me alone, I keep it still."

She was unable to resist when he touched her forehead with the agate. Numbness invaded her mind, her body.

"I want you to invite me into your house, Inary."
Roy's words crawled like worms into her ears.

Though in some deep inner core she knew she must
never invite him across her threshold, she heard herself say, mindless as a robot, "Please come inside,
Roy."

He plucked the key from her unresisting fingers,
unlocked the door and opened it. She was dimly aware
of the cats scooting past her into the house before he
gestured for her to enter and followed her in. He
closed the door behind them and she heard him click
the lock.

He ushered her into the living room as though he,
not she, owned the house. "Sit on the couch," he ordered. She found she had no choice but to obey.

Roy prowled through the downstairs, looking,
touching, turning on a light here and there, and,
though somewhere within her she felt the violation
keenly, she was powerless to stop him. He started up
the stairs, paused and picked up something—she
couldn't see what—then stopped. Turning around, he
came back to her.

"First things first," he said, smiling as he sat beside her.

Her gaze fixed on the pendant he held in his fingers, on the agate embedded in the crystal. He swayed
it back and forth in front of her, the crystal catching
the light, sparkling, dazzling her.

"Like the agate trapped in the crystal," he murmured, "you're caught within my spell. You belong to
me—everything you know, everything you are."

As her surroundings faded, she was conscious he
continued to speak softly, but her sense of his words
faded and vanished. There was only the agate, once

hers, freely given to him. Offered without the realization she'd be giving herself away with the stone. Inary's world shrank to a dazzle of light....

When she came to partial awareness again, she found herself in Roy's arms, his lips pressed against hers. The untouched core within her shrank with loathing, but her body responded, clinging to him, returning his kiss. She belonged to Roy, belonged to him forever.

No. Use your power. Fight!

How could she? He controlled her will.

His caresses grew more intimate, touching her bared flesh, and though she made no attempt to pull away, her inner resistance flared. Help me! she begged silently, not certain who or what she was asking.

Faint and far away, she heard a voice and tried desperately to focus on it, to call the voice to her. Whose was it? Aunt Inary's?

"Time goes in," the voice chanted, closer now, repeating words Inary had heard before, years ago, words her aunt had intoned on Agate Point, the words that had vanquished a younger Roy.

Concentrating, straining to free one hand, Inary reached into the pocket of her jeans and pulled out a tiny rose sachet. Clutching it tightly in one hand, she forced her aunt's chant from her unwilling lips:

"Time goes in

"Time goes out

"The rose within

"Locks darkness out."

Full awareness washed over Inary with the force of one of Superior's icy storm waves. She shuddered in Roy's embrace. "No!" she cried. "No! Let me go."

His grip tightened. "Too late," he said hoarsely. "Too little, too late."

No longer responding to him in any way, she writhed and twisted, trying to free herself. But, as his power had been stronger than hers, so was his physical strength. Though she struggled as hard as she could, she was no match for him. She couldn't prevent what he meant to do. He pinned her underneath him on the couch and tugged at her jeans.

There was no one to help her. Her aunt's words had released her from her compulsion, but she was still Roy's prisoner. Even if Ford realized she needed him, he was at Sweetgrass and could never return in time. Besides, Roy had locked the door.

Where was this power she was supposed to have? Why couldn't she summon it to her aid? The scarlet petals of the poppy blossomed in her mind, the darkness at its center turning to Roy's face. But the coil of energy she'd felt before didn't come to her. She was helpless.

She heard a low, steady growl—a roaring in her ears?—and suddenly Roy yelled and flung himself away from her, cursing and grabbing at his head. Inary stared with amazement at Gilgamesh, who clung precariously to Roy's head, one of his hind claws digging bloody furrows in Roy's cheek.

She scrambled off the couch, yanking up her jeans, but before she could try to help the cat, Roy flung Gilgamesh away from him and grabbed for her.

"That's enough!" Ford's voice rang out loud and clear as he strode into the living room from the entry. He paused to scoop up the dazed Gilgamesh and thrust the cat into Inary's arms. Standing between her and Roy, he said, "Get out, Nuhaim."

This time there was no mistaking the power crackling through the room. Inary could feel its sizzle as the two men confronted one another.

"She's mine, Werlich," Roy snarled. "No matter what you do, she's mine."

"No." Ford spoke flatly.

Inary cuddled the cat against her bare breasts, vehemently agreeing with Ford. She was *not* Roy's. She would never be his. She didn't belong to anyone but herself.

Something spoke from deep within her. *You can't be yourself until you free your power.*

Shaken, she retreated until she could lean against a wall for support.

"You haven't won, Werlich," Roy said. "I'll be back. You know that, don't you?"

"Get out," Ford repeated.

"I'm going. For now." Roy looked past Ford to Inary. "Werlich can't protect you," he told her. "No one can—not he nor your cats. Nothing can save you." He turned on his heel and swaggered from the house.

Exhausted, feeling as though she'd been drained of every atom of energy, Inary sank onto the couch, still clutching Gilgamesh to her. She heard Ford lock and bolt the door behind Roy, then watched him return.

"Get dressed," he said coldly, without looking at her.

She set the cat beside her, noting with relief that he seemed more stunned than hurt, and pulled on her T-shirt. As she slid into her cotton knit jacket, Enkidu appeared from behind the couch, jumped up and began licking Gilgamesh.

"I warned you not to invite him into your house," Ford said without turning around.

"I'm dressed," she said wearily, stroking Gilgamesh.

He turned to look at her. "Why did you?" he asked.

"After he showed me a pendant with an agate set into it, the agate I gave him a long time ago, I had no control over what I said or did." She spoke in a monotone, past caring what Ford or anyone else thought. Despite the jacket, she felt icy cold.

He stared down at her without saying anything. She remained silent. Enkidu looked up at Ford, leapt off the couch and peered underneath it to bat at something. The crystal pendant on its gold chain rolled into view.

Ford retrieved it, carefully examining the agate embedded in the crystal. "The chain's broken," he said.

"That must have happened when Gilgamesh attacked Roy," she told him.

Ford leaned down and touched Gilgamesh's head. "A brave guardian," he said. Seating himself on the couch with the cats between them, he handed her the pendant. "Because your cat took back the agate, Roy's hold over you is broken."

She gazed at the pendant and shuddered. Ford's hand closed over hers, warming her, his strength revitalizing her.

"I apologize for accusing you of inviting Roy in. I should have known you had no choice." He sighed. "It's unfortunate but it couldn't be helped. You do realize he no longer needs to be invited in—he can enter at will. So now more than ever it's vitally necessary to keep everything locked."

Inary, beginning to feel more like herself, sat up straighter and ran a hand through her hair. "How did *you* get in?" she asked. "I was sure he locked the door."

"I admit I kept back a spare key."

She pulled her hand free. "What? After you assured me you'd given me all the house keys?"

He had the grace to look abashed. "My only excuse is that I thought I might need to use the key in an emergency." He reached in his pocket and gave her the key. "You have my word I don't have another."

Inary's brief flare of annoyance faded. "This certainly qualified as an emergency," she admitted as she gave him back the key. "I'll feel better knowing you have it. But how did you get here so fast from the hospital?"

"I wasn't there, I was home. I didn't have to go."

She blinked. "But I thought I heard your car."

"I started the car to make sure the ignition was working—I've had some trouble with it. As it was, I didn't know you needed me—that damned agate gave him too much power—until you somehow broke through to me."

"Aunt Inary helped me. But I wasn't strong enough to fight him off. He almost—" She stopped, unable to go on.

Ford lifted the cats from between them and gathered her into his arms, holding her gently, comfortingly. "It took the four of us—you, the cats and me," he said, "but we prevailed. With, I gather, a bit of aid from your aunt. You're safe. For now."

Safe. The word echoed in her ears. Yes, for the moment. But as hard as he might try to protect her, Ford's arms offered only the illusion of safety. Her only chance to remain safe lay within herself. How could she find the key to unlock her power? She was grimly aware it wouldn't be tonight—she was almost too tired to think at all.

"Don't leave me alone," she whispered.

"I won't," he assured her. "I didn't intend to, even before you mentioned it. I'll call the hospital and give them your number so they can reach me."

She pushed away from him in alarm. "What if you're called and have to go?"

He smiled at her. "No problem. If I have to go, you'll come with me. Otherwise I'll sleep in the guest bedroom, just down the hall from you."

In her own bed, Inary, knowing Ford was close at hand, fell asleep immediately.

She woke in the morning, still caught in the web of a dream where she'd searched and searched for something she'd forgotten, not knowing exactly what she looked for but aware she must find it or disaster would overtake her.

What could it be? she asked herself, unable to extricate herself fully from the dream's clinging strands. Then she realized the cats weren't on the bed with her as they always were in the morning and she sat up abruptly.

The smell of coffee triggered her memory. Ford had spent the night. He must have let the cats out for their morning run. And the sun was shining. Smiling, her worrisome dream dismissed, she trailed into the bathroom.

After breakfast, Ford insisted they leave the dishes in the sink. "Why waste a beautiful morning?" he asked. "God knows we get few enough of them in the U.P. We'll take a walk."

"But," she protested, "don't you have to go to work?"

He shook his head. "I've rearranged my schedule for today so I'll be working the same hours you are. That way we can drive to the hospital and back together."

For a moment she was pleased and then she saw the other, darker side. "You can't believe I'd be in any danger at Sweetgrass," she said.

"With three days left until Walpurgis Night, why take chances? You haven't asked me but I plan to be your guest through the night of April 30."

"I certainly don't object."

He waited until they were walking along the water's edge to say, "After tonight, I think you ought to stay home instead of going to work on Saturday and Sunday."

She stared at him. "Not go to work? I just started at the hospital, I can't afford to not show up when I'm scheduled to be on duty. Anyway, I can't see the point of it. Who's going to threaten me while I'm on C2? There's always a guard patrolling the parking lot when I go off duty and when I come home you'll be here waiting, won't you?"

"Yes, but—" He shook his head. "I suppose I could drive you and pick you up."

Inary stopped walking and faced him, her mind made up. "Definitely not. I'll drive myself. Actually, I'd feel safer with you here in my house while I'm gone."

"You have a point," he admitted. "Nuhaim can't very well break into the house while I'm inside."

She drew in her breath. "Do you think he'll try?"

"It depends on whether he knows about the room in the attic. Once he was invited in, your house is no longer impregnable as far as he's concerned. If the doors are locked, which they certainly will be—and bolted besides—he might try to force his way in if he thought no one was home."

"In the grimoire, my aunt mentions seekers-of-darkness bothering her because of the pentacle."

"Yes, she told me about the seekers, if not the pentacle. If others knew the pentacle exists, Nuhaim could have learned of it. I think you're right when you say I should remain in the house, but I'm still unhappy about you working the last two evenings of this month."

"I'd *rather* work than sit around at home worrying." She reached down, selected a flat stone and skimmed it across the water, watching it skip three times before sinking. "Three jumps. That's good luck."

Ford put his arm over her shoulders. "Let's hope so. We're going to need it."

CHAPTER TWELVE

Inary turned from Ford to look at the lake. Superior's blue water, bright with sunlight, stretched as far as she could see. In the distance, a thin smear of smoke told of a passing boat, probably an ore boat, too far away to be visible.

Up the beach, a single long-legged sandpiper ran along the waterline, leaving delicate footprints on the damp sand. Plaintive birdcalls from somewhere above her made Inary glance up. High in the sky, a vee of wild geese winged northward.

She raised both her arms as though to salute their passage. "This is all so beautiful!" she cried.

"I know." Ford spoke quietly. "The surroundings are what keep me here despite the many months of rotten weather."

"But now it's spring," she said. "Though there may be a few patches of snow left in the deep woods, the trees are leafing out and I found pussy willows near the swamp earlier in the week. Winter's back is broken."

He smiled at her. "You don't have to convince me. Spring surrounds us—I can smell its freshness in the air, I can hear it in the courting calls of the birds."

"Spring is a time of renewal, of awakening. A time of brightness. Why should the dark threaten anyone this time of the year? In the past, what made them choose April to celebrate Walpurgis Night?"

"In the old days some called it Beltain and set the date as May 1. The ancients didn't actually celebrate spring on those days. What they tried to do was placate the gods by human sacrifice to guarantee the arrival of spring each year, to ensure the end of winter's blight, to exchange the dark for the light."

"At least we've made some advances since then," she said.

"In some ways."

Just as a passing cloud momentarily hid the sun, the sandpiper, finding itself stalked by Gilgamesh, flew away.

"When the sun would pop in and out of the clouds like this," Inary said, "my aunt used to tell me we were having a patchy day. She believed life was the same—patches of light alternating with patches of dark, laughter one day, sadness the next."

"What did she have to say about rain?" he asked.

Inary smiled. "April showers bring May flowers." Glancing down at the sand, she scuffed aside a few pebbles with the toe of her shoe and stooped to pick up a white stone She studied it, then tossed it away. "I thought that one might be a white agate, but it doesn't have the markings."

"Which reminds me," he said. "What did you do with the agate in the crystal? Though I think Nuhaim's hold over you has been broken for good, I wouldn't want him to get his hands on that agate again."

"I hid it in my aunt's special place. Neither he nor anyone else will ever find the pendant." For some reason her words reminded her of the dream she'd had about forgetting something, but, though she tried hard, she could make no connection between the dream and what she'd just said.

Ford grasped her hand and drew her away from the beach into the pines. Once they were surrounded by the tall trees whose needled branches formed a canopy overhead, he stopped and put his hands on her shoulders.

"I wanted to kill Nuhaim last night," he said. "When I saw him touching you against your will, trying to force you—" He shook his head. "I've spent years learning how the forces of heredity and environment shape us, twisting some of us into malevolence. I've spent years more trying to undo the damage, believing it could be undone. Gradually I've come to understand and to accept that not everyone can be helped, and the truly dangerous can only be locked away where they can't harm others.

"In Nuhaim's case, even locking him up is no solution. He's far too powerful. The only way to prevent Nuhaim from injuring others—" Again he paused, finally adding, "I've never thought of myself as a killer—I thought it would be impossible for me to deliberately kill anyone, even though I was once responsible for a man's death. He died because of my ignorance, not because I meant to kill him. What happened to that man haunts me still. I was so certain I knew myself through and through, and yet last night, if I'd been armed, I might well have become a deliberate killer. Which goes to show you how imperfect psychiatry is. And also how imperfect the power of witchcraft is."

"Or maybe it goes to show how much of a menace Roy Nuhaim is," she corrected, unhappy to see Ford so upset. "In any case, you didn't kill him."

Ford held her gaze, his dark eyes burning with fervor. "I won't let him harm you. Never again. I swear it." He pulled her close, wrapping his arms around her, his lips meeting hers with a fierce intensity.

She clung to him, responding with a passion that matched his, and was beginning to shut out everything else when she heard Enkidu's mournful yowls. Ford must have heard the cat at the same time, because he released her and looked around.

Enkidu sat by the trunk of a nearby pine, watching them, no longer yowling. Ford smiled one-sidedly. "I think he means, 'This is your first warning—quit or next we send in the attack cat.'"

She glanced between the trees but there was no sign of Gilgamesh. "We were only kissing," she protested.

"Between us there's no such thing as 'only' kissing, and the cats know it. So do you. So do I. And yet I can't seem to stop. Maybe we should try something else." He bent and rubbed noses with her. "Enkidu certainly can't object to that. Unfortunately it doesn't come close to what I'd like to do with you."

Inary laughed. "It's all we *can* do while our chaperons are watching." Taking his hand, she started back to the beach.

Later, when they were ready to leave for Sweetgrass, Ford insisted she leave the cats outside.

"But I don't like them out after dark. It's dangerous."

"Cats are nocturnal animals by nature," he said. "In the wild they hunt by dark. They'll get along without difficulty even though you've trained them to stay in at night. I have a particular reason for wanting them outside when we come home tonight. I'll be able to tell by their behavior if it's safe to enter your house."

She stared at him. "You think it might not be safe?"

"I don't know. The cats will tell me."

Though she dropped her objection, Inary worried about the cats as they drove to the hospital in her car after leaving his at a garage in Norwich to have the ignition checked. She dropped him off at one of the adult units and parked in the lot nearest to C2.

Wheatie was on duty and, after they'd gone through the change-of-shift routine, she said to Inary, "I heard you've been trying something new with Sunny that the evening nurse assistants swear helps to control her. We could sure use help with Sunny on days."

"It's just the laying on of hands."

"Yeah? I've seen the technique demonstrated but never tried it. Does it really work?"

"Sometimes," Inary replied cautiously.

"Maybe you could show us. I'll bet Laine would be interested, too. Would you?"

Inary thought quickly, not wanting to get involved, particularly since she was a new employee, in something the director of nurses might not approve of. Anyway, she wasn't at all sure she was the right person to teach the laying on of hands.

"I've got a better idea," she said. "Why don't you get together with Laine, and the two of you put in a formal request for a class to be taught at Sweetgrass on the theory and technique? It might be of benefit to other nurses and nurse assistants."

"Hey, that's a good idea. The front office is always asking us charge nurses for suggestions for courses we'd like to take."

When Ford came on to her unit shortly after eight, Inary took him into Mouse's room to forestall the little girl from getting out of bed to see him. Since Mouse's room was relatively private even though shared with other children, while Ford held Mouse in his arms, Inary told him what Wheatie had wanted.

"You made a good decision," he said. "You can't be sure your success with Sunny isn't partly due to your developing power."

"I don't feel my power developing," she said.

"I do. But I wish you knew how to hurry it along."

Mouse reached over and grasped one of Inary's hands. Solemnly she placed Inary's hand on Ford's, then looked from one to the other and smiled.

"You got that right, Mouse," he said, giving the child a hug. "Time for you to go back to bed. Once you're tucked in, I'll tell you a story about two cats— a gray-and-white cat and a black long-haired cat with only three paws."

Smiling, Inary left him putting Mouse back in her railed bed. Sometime later, Ford caught up to her as she was checking on Rocky to make sure the boy wasn't convulsing. He waited in the doorway until she'd finished and then she walked with him along the hall to the door leading out of C2, where he paused.

"Do you think Mouse will ever be able to leave Sweetgrass?" she asked.

He sighed. "She came here from a foster home because the foster mother felt she couldn't cope with Mouse. I gather Mouse's real home situation was impossible, which was why she was in foster care to begin with. If she could leave, where would she go?"

"There must be someplace better than this for her."

"We have to work with her first. Only after that can we make any decision about her future. And we can't begin working with her until you're ready."

Inary wanted to insist she was always ready to help Mouse, but she held back her words, knowing he meant she needed to gain full use of her power.

"Even when you're capable of working with me," he added, "we'll have to go slowly. We'll have to be very, very careful."

She nodded, all too aware of his reason. Mouse must not be harmed by anything either of them did.

Ford left, but at the end of her shift, came back to meet her at the door, causing the C2 nurse assistants to raise their eyebrows. It'll be all over the hospital by tomorrow, Inary thought resignedly.

The ride home was uneventful. As she maneuvered her car along the sandy drive, Ford rolled down his window and listened. For what, she wasn't sure. The moon was up, two days from full, she recalled, and her house looked strangely unfamiliar in its silvery light. She parked and reached for the door handle.

Ford gripped her arm, saying, "Wait. The cats should have come running when they heard the car. I expected them to be on the porch already, waiting to be let in. They're not, and I don't see them. Something's wrong."

Inary tensed, peering into the moonlit night and listening. "I hear one of them," she said after a moment.

Ford craned his neck out the car window. "It's Gilgamesh. He's up in the rowan tree. Alone. Don't leave the car. Call him and see if he'll climb down."

Did the cats know the rowan was a tree that protects? she wondered. Though she was on the wrong side of the car to be able to look up into the tree, she called Gilgamesh, coaxing him to come to her. For long moments nothing happened.

"He's starting down," Ford reported finally. "We can leave the car."

He prowled around the outside of the house with a flashlight while she encouraged the cat from the bottom of the tree. Gilgamesh slowly worked his way from branch to branch, at last jumping into her arms from the lowest limb. He hooked his claws into her jacket, clinging desperately to her, his body shaking with tremors.

"I've got him," she called to Ford, seeing him standing on the porch.

"How is he?"

"Something really must have scared him," she said as, carrying Gilgamesh, she hurried to join Ford. About to ask him if he'd seen any sign of Enkidu, she swallowed the words, drawing in her breath when she noticed the limp body Ford held.

"Is he— Is he—?" She couldn't bring herself to finish the question.

"I can feel a faint heartbeat—he's alive. I can't find any injuries, but he's in shock."

"You told me to leave them outside," she accused. "You said they'd be all right."

"Open the door."

Shifting Gilgamesh so she could reach her key, she obeyed. Moments later she sat in the rocker by the fireplace with both cats in her lap while Ford lit the fire he'd laid earlier. As flames licked up around the logs, Gilgamesh began to lick Enkidu's fur.

Ford crouched beside the rocker, running his hands over Enkidu. "No broken bones. He must have been frightened into a state of shock."

"By what?"

"Nuhaim. The cats must have sensed something darker within him than I suspected." He shook his head. "I thought the cats would hide from danger. Or climb the rowan if they had to. I didn't allow for Enkidu's lost paw—evidently he couldn't reach the tree as quickly as Gilgamesh." He lifted Enkidu from her lap, cradling the cat in his arms as he sat on the raised hearth bricks.

"They'd have been safe inside," she pointed out crossly.

"If they had been, we wouldn't have known Nuhaim was here."

"We still don't know!" she cried. "It might have been a stray dog or a bear or some other wild animal that went after the cats."

Ford shook his head. "It wasn't an animal. Enkidu wasn't savaged—he hasn't a mark on him. Nuhaim was here scouting, looking for a way in. He didn't find one but he scared the hell out of the cats."

Enkidu whimpered, his body twitching. Gilgamesh leaped from Inary's lap and jumped up beside Ford where he resumed licking Enkidu.

"He's coming around," Ford said. "In less than an hour he'll be back to normal. Cats are hardy."

"I absolutely refuse to leave them out after dark again."

"We won't need to. I'll be here the next two nights to stand off Nuhaim, and they'll be inside with me."

Enkidu's eyes opened and he shifted position in Ford's arms. "You're safe, hairy one," Ford murmured. "We'll try to keep you safe from now on."

By the time Inary was ready to go to bed, Enkidu, as Ford had predicted, was able to walk around under his own power. Later, when he curled up with Gilgamesh on her bed, he even purred.

Inary woke to the smell of coffee and the nagging feeling she'd had the same dream of searching for something unknown. Downstairs, she found both cats as frisky as ever.

"I went out with them earlier," Ford reported. "Enkidu behaved as though nothing had ever frightened him. The weather's changed, though. Feels like rain."

"You don't have to sit inside with me all morning," she told him after breakfast. "In fact, since I intend to clean the house, you'll be in the way."

"I can take a hint when I'm hit over the head with one. I'll take the cats for another walk, bring them back and then go home until you're ready to go to work. How's that?"

The house did need cleaning, but not urgently. Inary dusted and mopped and vacuumed to keep her mind off the vague peril lurking in the darkness of the next two nights, concentrating on what she was doing to the exclusion of anything else. When the cats returned, she was surprised to see their fur was damp.

As they hurried to sit in front of the fireplace and lick themselves dry, she noticed rain slanting across the windows. The wind had risen; she could hear it moan around the house corners. Though it wasn't quite one o'clock, the day had taken on the gloom of a winter afternoon. Where had spring gone?

Finding herself reluctant to don her uniform, Inary was forced to acknowledge her lack of desire for heading out into the depressing day. She grimaced and made herself get ready.

Ford arrived in a raincoat, started to kiss her good-bye, then grinned and rubbed noses with her instead.

As she drove along the highway, she felt trapped inside the car. Her windshield wipers competed futilely with the gusting rain and the road to Sweetgrass seemed endless. She found herself fighting down a rising apprehension, as though her final destination, instead of being the hospital, was unknown.

Arriving in the parking lot at last, she looked for her umbrella and discovered she'd forgotten it. Sighing in exasperation, she ran through the rain, getting her uniform pants so wet they clung to her legs by the time she reached the building. What else can go wrong? she asked herself gloomily.

Mouse, waiting inside the door, pounced on Inary the minute she entered C2, clinging to her hand and pressing against her dripping raincoat. When Inary went into the nurses' station for the end-of-shift report, Mouse huddled outside the closed half door, waiting.

When she finally had time to spend a few moments paying attention to Mouse, Inary did her best to discover what had upset the child. But Mouse didn't seem able to summon up any pictures of what might be troubling her and she continued to try to cling, which threw Inary's routine off, making her run late all evening.

Whether because of Mouse's agitation or Inary's distraction due to it, or something else entirely, every child on the unit seemed affected. They spent the first few hours of the shift acting out their upset and creating one minor problem after another.

Rocky took off his helmet and threw it at Mary Johnson, Sammy vomited his evening meal all over Goldie and himself, the younger children wailed peevishly, several of the older ones hit each other, and Sunny, behaving like some wild animal, got her mask off and bit Erma's arm severely, earning an involuntary whack from the startled nurse assistant.

Since Erma was a big woman, her cuff toppled Sunny, who cut her head in the fall, a scalp wound that bled profusely. Sunny had to be restrained within a sheet and also have her head held to allow Inary to clean the injury and determine how serious it was. Fortunately, the gash was a small one, making stitches unnecessary, so a doctor didn't have to be called.

Erma, though, had to leave the unit to have her bite checked by the supervisor. He decided she needed a doctor's treatment, so Erma was off the unit for over an hour, leaving Mary Johnson and Inary shorthanded at their busiest time.

They were late getting the children fed, Inary was behind with her evening medications and, by the time Erma returned with her arm bandaged, they were late putting the children to bed.

Before she could concentrate on Mouse, Inary had to write up, in triplicate, an incident report about what had happened to Erma and to Sunny.

"I swear I didn't mean to hit her," Erma said. "I never hit one of the kids before. It was sort of a reflex, you know? Like my hand went out before I could stop it." She stared unhappily at Inary. "You think I might lose my job over this?"

"Not if I can help it," Inary said. "I know you wouldn't deliberately hurt any of our kids."

After administering a sedative to the restrained but thrashing and struggling Sunny, Inary found it impossible to even try to attempt the laying on of hands. Both she and Sunny were far too disturbed.

At last Inary was able to look in on Mouse, huddled in her bed but not asleep. She brought a pad of paper and the carton of colored markers she'd given Mouse and persuaded the child to sit up. Handing Mouse the carton of colored markers, she laid the pad of paper on the bed.

"Draw something for me," she coaxed, hoping Mouse might be able to express herself this way.

Mouse looked at her, then at the paper. She opened the carton and studied the markers, choosing one. Pressing the point to the paper, she began streaking the black marker across the white paper, finally completely covering the sheet with darkness. She tore it from the pad and offered it to Inary.

Inary bit her lip. "Oh, Mouse," she cried, lifting the child from the bed and sitting in the chair next to it. She cuddled Mouse in her arms, crooning to her, doing her best to calm both the little girl and herself.

Mary looked in on her once. Inary raised questioning eyebrows, but Mary shook her head, indicating there was nothing urgent. When she felt Mouse relax in her arms, Inary rose and carefully tucked the child into her bed.

Back at the nurses' station, she sat down and belatedly started her evening charting, barely finishing by the end of the shift.

It was still raining when she slid damply into her car and left the parking lot. Again the drive seemed interminable. The road and the rain will never end, she thought gloomily. I'm doomed to drive on and on forever, never reaching home.

Preoccupied with a rehash of the evening's confusion, Inary almost missed the turnoff to her house, yanking the wheel so sharply at the last minute that her car skidded across the road. Luckily there wasn't another car in sight. She turned in the right direction and sighed in relief when she pulled up in front of her house.

Ford had the porch light on, and before she got out of the car, he'd opened the front door. Seeing him framed in the light was such a welcome sight that Inary, forgetful of their tacit agreement, flung herself into his arms.

He shut the door, still holding her, then drew her closer. To her surprise and distress, she burst into tears.

"I've had enough," she sobbed. "I just want to be left alone."

"You mean you don't want me here?" he asked, easing away enough to look at her.

"It's not you, it's everything else!" she wailed.

She heard him reach to bolt the door, then he led her into the living room, took off her wet coat and pulled her down onto the couch with him, cuddling her on his lap. The cats jumped up to join them, crowding close. One of them licked her hand.

Nothing had been solved, nothing at all, but, somehow, she felt immeasurably better and her tears stopped. She wiped her face with a tissue from her pocket, took a deep breath and let it out slowly.

"Bad time at work?" Ford asked.

Leaning her head against his chest, she told him just how bad. "I think it all began because Mouse was so upset," she finished. "Is it possible she could affect the entire unit?"

"I'm not sure exactly what abilities she has, but I'd say she probably could. What upset her?"

"Me. Or at least that's what I'm beginning to believe. Look at this." Inary eased a folded paper from her pocket.

Ford frowned at the scribbled blackness. "First she drew a poppy, now this. I'm afraid you're right. Mouse senses the darkness threatening you and she's frightened. She's likely to still be troubled when you go to work tomorrow evening."

"How can I possibly reassure her?"

"By using your power."

Inary slid off his lap, almost squashing Enkidu, who protested. She rescued the cat, holding him as she stood looking down at Ford. "It's hopeless," she said. "I'll never learn."

"Put the athame under your pillow tonight," he said. "The knife must still hold some of your aunt's power and maybe you'll dream."

"What good are dreams? For two nights now I've dreamed this same dream where I'm searching desperately for something unknown, something I've forgotten. In the dream, if I don't find whatever it is, something terrible will happen. If that doesn't mean I'm searching for how to use my power, what does it mean?"

"Something you've forgotten?" he repeated, frowning as he got to his feet.

She nodded.

"I don't think you've interpreted the dream correctly," he said. "I don't think it has anything to do with a search for your power. It's possible there *is* something important you've forgotten."

"What?"

"Could Nuhaim have used that crystal to hypnotize you?" Ford seemed to be asking himself as much as her.

Inary tried to recall exactly what had happened on that horrible night Roy had entered her house, and found she wasn't quite sure. The evening seemed strangely, disturbingly blurred in her mind.

"Nuhaim might have." As he answered his own question, Ford gazed intently at Inary. "He could have. Since your aunt hypnotized you as a child, you're probably quite susceptible."

Inary shuddered, feeling violated by the very idea of being hypnotized.

"But even if he did," Ford went on, "what could Nuhaim want you to forget?"

CHAPTER THIRTEEN

Inary woke before dawn. She could no longer hear rain beating against the window, and the wind had ceased its moaning. Though the cats still seemed to be sleeping, unalarmed, she was certain something had roused her. Feeling the hair rise on her nape, she stared into the room's darkness, listening.

"Inary." When the voice spoke, she tensed but the cats slept on. Then she realized the voice—her aunt's voice—was in her head.

"Inary, child, your power lies under your pillow. Bring it forth."

Inary reached under her pillow, gripped the handle of the athame and drew the knife free.

"The athame is yours," her aunt whispered, "freely given as it was to me. Within the knife lies the secret of your power. Within your belief lies the use of your power. Strengthen your belief and, when the moon next rises, bind the athame to you by blood and by the moon. So I say to you and so might it be."

Inary's sense of a presence in the room faded. She waited, but when nothing more happened, she eased the knife under her pillow once more. The cats shifted position and she put a hand on each of them for comfort, certain she'd never be able to go back to sleep.

The next she knew, sun was streaming in through her windows and the cats were gone. Inary sat up in bed. Had she dreamed the voice or had her aunt actually spoken to her in the early morning hours? She lifted the pillow and gazed at the athame.

The knife lay on the white sheet, its daggerlike blade slim and tapered, the inlaid ebony crescents dark against the silver handle. Her hand curled about the hilt. *Hers. Freely given.*

She slid from the bed, knife in hand, and padded to the window to look at the sky. Nearly cloudless. No clouds to hide the moon tonight. The full moon, whose light would shine on good and evil alike.

Wrapping the athame in the red silk, she laid it on the dresser. The room seemed stuffy, so she raised one of the windows over the porch a few inches, only to be confronted by the closed storm window beyond.

Recalling her aunt's ritual every May, she thought, I'll have to see about taking the storm windows off and putting the screens on. Ford said he'd show me how. And I really ought to think about replacing these old storm windows with more modern double-duty storm-screen sashes. If I can afford it.

For the moment, though, she merely unhooked the storm window and swung it open at the bottom, holding it in place with its attached metal rod. Fresh, cool air streamed into the bedroom, air smelling of spring. Inary closed her eyes and breathed deeply.

Before she went downstairs, she shut the inside window almost all the way, leaving just a crack to admit fresh air. At breakfast, she expected Ford to ask if she'd dreamed, but he didn't. When she tried to tell him about her aunt's voice in the night, the words stuck in her throat, so she said nothing about it.

Do I really believe I can stand under the moon tonight with the athame and ask for power? she wondered. On the other hand, do I have any choice?

"I have some things to do at home," Ford said when they finished breakfast. "I'll come back before you leave."

She nodded. Actually she was relieved to have some time alone. Though there was no one in the world she'd rather be with than Ford, she needed to come to grips with what she meant to do. She needed to make a decision that no one could help her with.

The cats accompanying her, she walked to the beach. There she sat on a driftwood log gazing at the lake, soothed by the constant wash of the waves onto the sand and all but mesmerized by the sunlight's glitter on the water. Never before had she felt so attuned to a place.

This is my home, this is where I belong, she told herself. No one can drive me away. If I must, I'll fight to stay here.

Later, as she walked along the waterline, she grew so warm she shucked her jacket, enjoying the sun's heat on her bare arms. It was too nice a day to be inside, and she delayed getting ready to go to work until after one-thirty.

"The thermometer's up to sixty-eight," Ford told her when he returned to her house shortly before two, wearing a T-shirt and jeans. "Summer weather. Warm enough to take some of your C2 kids outside."

"That's a great idea," she said. "We haven't been using the fenced yard on the evening shift because the evenings have been too chilly."

"My suggestion is to separate the more active children from Mouse if you find she's still agitated. Let the nurse assistants watch them outside while you stay in and do what you can to soothe Mouse."

She nodded, believing his plan might well prevent another chaotic evening. "Nothing I tried with Mouse last night calmed her," she said. "I'm fresh out of ideas on what to try next."

"Give me a minute or two and I'll try to come up with something."

While he was thinking, Inary sliced the apricot-nut bread she'd made the day before and wrapped the slices to take to work since it was her turn to bring goodies. She slung her bag over her shoulder and tried to think of anything she might have forgotten.

The athame. Should she bring it with her?

Now or never, she told herself, hurrying upstairs and stuffing the silk-wrapped knife into her commodious bag. When she came back down, Ford was standing in the entry.

"Make up a story for Mouse," he said. "A story where someone like you is in danger and overcomes it so there's a happy ending." He spread his hands. "It might or might not do the trick, but it's worth a try."

Pleased, she smiled. "I'd never have thought of that. I guess shrinks are of some use, after all."

"You've only begun to tap my resources."

"Is that so? What kind of resources?"

He grinned at her. "If it weren't for the fact that Gilgamesh is sitting on the stairs watching me and that you're going to be late if you don't leave within a few minutes, I'd be happy to offer a few selective samples."

But at the door, his smile faded, his expression becoming grim. "Be careful, Inary. Be very careful tonight." He cupped her face in his hands and kissed her.

It never occurred to her to tell him to be careful. She knew Ford had powers she didn't understand, powers he was well able to use. She was certain he could take care of himself, even on Walpurgis Night.

Anyway, maybe all this worry and fuss was for no good reason. Maybe nothing unusual would happen. Hadn't Roy tried and failed to break into her house? With Ford on guard, Roy was sure to fail again if he tried.

C2 was in an uproar when Inary arrived.

"We just found out Dorothy Marten is missing," Wheatie told her. "There's no way we can figure she could have gotten off the unit, and yet we can't find her."

It took Inary a moment to realize Wheatie was talking about Mouse. "I'll help look," she said. "Where have you searched already?"

"She's not outside in the fenced yard, in any of the patient rooms, bathrooms, linen closet or dayroom."

"What about the storage closet and exam room?"

"They're locked and they have been all during my shift—how could she get in?"

"I don't know," Inary said, "but if you'll give me the unit keys, I'll look in those rooms, anyway."

"Ray's got the storage closet key." As she handed Inary the other keys, Wheatie called to the day-shift LPN, asking him to look inside the closet.

Inary hurried to the exam room, unlocked it and switched on the light. She drew in her breath as she stared at a drawing on the tile floor, a drawing in bright red of a crude but unmistakable five-pointed star surrounded by a circle. A pentacle. In the center of the pentacle, the red marking pen sat balanced upright on its cap.

"Mouse!" she cried, peering around the room.

Mouse huddled in a corner behind the trash can, head down, hair over her face. Inary shoved the can aside and knelt beside her.

"I'm here," she said softly. "And you can see I'm safe. This is no place for you to be."

Mouse flung herself at Inary, wrapping her arms and legs around her and holding her so tightly it was an effort for Inary to get to her feet. With one arm around Mouse, she quickly searched the room to make certain the little girl hadn't gotten into anything that might harm her, but nothing had been disturbed. Inary flicked off the light and left the room, the door locking automatically as it closed.

Wheatie was talking on the phone when Inary came into the nurses' station, still holding Mouse.

"—no, we haven't, not yet," Wheatie was saying when she saw Inary. "Wait! Yes, we've found her. She's right here. No, I don't think she's hurt."

"Mouse—Dorothy, I mean—is fine," Inary assured Wheatie. "Somehow she got trapped in the exam room and didn't know how to get out."

Wheatie relayed the information to the front office and hung up. "How the devil did she get in there?" she asked herself as much as Inary. "I didn't unlock the door all shift and neither did Ray."

"Yeah, but Dr. Thomas came on the unit while you were at lunch," Ray put in from the medicine room. "I didn't see him go in the exam room, but he could have—all the doctors have keys."

Wheatie sighed. "I'll write the incident report that way, otherwise it won't make sense. I suppose it's possible Dorothy scooted in behind the doctor and hid so he didn't realize she was there. She's very good at hiding. Dorothy didn't touch anything while she was in there, did she? I mean, like drink something poisonous?''

Inary shook her head. "I checked."

"Well, thank God it wasn't any worse."

Since any attempt to loosen Mouse's grip made the child cling even tighter, Inary went through the change-of-shift routine holding her.

"You'll spoil that kid if you're not careful," Wheatie warned as she went off duty.

Before she began her evening routine, Inary sat down with Mouse on her lap. "I have to give the other children their medicine," she said. "And there are other important things I must do that I can't do while I'm carrying you. Do you understand?"

Mouse sniffled, tilting her head to peer at Inary's face.

"Here's what we're going to do. You're going to let go of me, and then I'll unroll some bandaging, tie it around my waist and leave a long piece for you to hold on to. That way we'll still be connected but I'll have my hands free. You can help by using my bandage scissors to cut off the right length from the roll, okay?"

Gently but firmly, Inary detached herself from Mouse and persuaded the girl to clutch the end of the bandage instead of hanging on to her.

After supper, Erma took some of the children, including Sunny, outside, and the unit quieted considerably. Later, when Inary, still trailed by Mouse, went in to see if she could help Sunny, the child had already drifted off to sleep.

After she'd gotten Mouse ready for bed, Inary had an inspiration. Since Mouse had drawn the pentacle, she'd tell a story about the pentacle, tell it to Mouse in the exam room and, in the telling, try to soothe Mouse's fear.

In the exam room, Inary filled a basin with warm water, placed it on the floor by the drawing and set a small stack of paper towels next to it. Then she sat on the exam table with Mouse on her lap.

"Once there was a girl named Irene who was a lot bigger and older than you," she said. "Irene had blond hair, like I do, and sort of yellow eyes, like a cat."

Mouse reached up and touched Inary's eyebrow, gazing solemnly into her eyes.

"Yes, Irene's eyes were like mine," Inary said. "Irene lived in a house that had a pentacle in the attic." She pointed to the drawing on the floor. "It was just like that one. Irene didn't know it, but a bad gnome lived inside the pentacle. He couldn't be seen and he couldn't get out, except for one night a year."

Mouse clutched Inary's arm.

"That night came, and the gnome started to break free. But Irene had two cats, a gray-and-white cat and a long-haired three-legged cat. These were magic cats and they knew about the gnome, so they came and got Irene out of bed and led her to the attic."

Inary, holding Mouse, slid off the table, crouched and picked up the capped red marker. "Irene had a magic wand, so we'll pretend this marker is her wand. When she realized that the gnome meant to come out of the pentacle and do bad things, she waved her magic wand like this."

Inary made an X in the air over the pentacle, set the marker aside and dipped several of the paper towels into the basin of water, thanking her lucky stars that she'd thought to buy washable markers for Mouse.

"Right after Irene waved her wand, the pentacle began to disappear, a little bit at a time." Inary wiped the wet towels over the drawing, discarding them when they became discolored and using fresh ones until at last all the red color had been washed from the tile floor.

"When the pentacle was gone," she finished, "so was the bad gnome, and he never bothered Irene or anyone else again."

Mouse stared for a long time at the damp floor, then turned to gaze at Inary. A picture slowly formed in Inary's mind—an image, she realized with amazement, of the athame.

"Yes," she told Mouse after taking a moment to collect her thoughts. "Yes, that's *my* magic wand."

Mouse, her small body still tense, continued to look at her. After a minute the image in Inary's mind changed. The knife turned so that its point was raised toward something round and shiny above it. Inary puzzled over the image. What did Mouse mean? Everything came, she believed, from her own mind, since she felt sure that was where the child found the images to begin with.

Then she realized Mouse could only mean the moon. The little girl was showing the athame raised to the moon. Inary bit her lip. Was Mouse telling her what she already knew—that the athame needed the moon to become magic?

"I know about the moon," she temporized.

The little girl's face puckered. Tears welled in her eyes.

"What is it?" Inary asked. "Do you want me to hold my wand up to the moon?"

Mouse blinked back the tears and smiled.

I have to do it, Inary decided. I can't promise Mouse I will otherwise. I have to go through the moon ritual for her sake.

"I promise I'll use the moon this very night," she said.

Mouse relaxed, going limp in her arms. But Inary couldn't relax. What had she committed herself to? It was true she'd brought the athame to work with her, but she hadn't actually decided to stand under the moon with it. Now she had to.

She started to leave the exam room, carrying Mouse, then paused to slide a sterile alcohol wipe, a disposable lancet and a dry cotton ball into her pocket. She'd need them for the ritual. The little girl made no objection to Inary putting her to bed and very quickly fell asleep.

When she left the unit after the change of shift, Inary walked quickly to the parking lot, more conscious than she'd ever been before of the moon's bright rays. As she drove from the hospital grounds in her car, the road leading away from Sweetgrass seemed to be a shining silver pathway beckoning her on. But, as she well knew, the road led only to home.

Where should she go through the ritual? Home might not be the best place, if Ford was right about the danger there. On the other hand, she hesitated to expose herself anywhere else. Should she wait until she reached home or not? Inary vacillated first one way, then the other, unable to make up her mind.

Not even halfway to Norwich, she suddenly found herself turning off onto a narrow, overgrown lane she could scarcely see in the moonlight, a lane that led into a stand of tall Scotch pines planted, she remembered Ford telling her, as a reforestation project by the CCC, the Civilian Conservation Corps.

These pines, planted long before either she or Ford were born, crowded close to her car, scraping against the sides and at last halting her passage. She turned off the motor but didn't leave the car.

Why did I turn here? she asked herself. Did I subconsciously notice the abandoned road while driving to work? Certainly her car was hidden from the highway, so no passing motorist could see it. But even so, why stop here, where the trees blocked the moonlight?

Hand on the key, ready to restart her car, Inary held, listening. It wasn't that she heard something, it was more of a mental summons, a calling without words. Under its spell, she eased from the car and, pushing branches aside, made her way through the pines until she came to a clearing, a small forest glade where spring-green plants, drained of color by the moon, had begun to flourish.

She felt no fear. She was alone but safe. The darkness under the surrounding trees was natural, not the breeding ground for evil. She hadn't so much chosen the spot as it had been chosen for her.

Now. Here. Begin. She thought it was her aunt's voice whispering in her head because she could feel Aunt Inary's presence very clearly, along with an eerie sensation that there were other intangible observers in the glade with her. But she wasn't afraid because, whoever or whatever they were, she knew they meant her no harm.

She spoke to her aunt without using words. *Little as I appreciated it, you tried to keep me safe when I was a child. You saved me from Roy, from an evil I was too young and foolish to comprehend, you left me a sanctuary to come home to. Forgive me for ever doubting you.*

A warmth crept over her, as though her aunt embraced her with love and forgiveness, something she'd never done while alive. Inary also understood her aunt would try, here and now, to help her accept and become what she was.

She hesitated only a moment before opening her bag and removing the silk-wrapped athame. Laying it carefully on the ground, she set her bag aside. Though she hadn't made a conscious decision until tonight to carry out the moon ritual, she realized that from the moment she'd first held the athame in her hand, this was meant to be.

She began by shedding her clothes, aware the supplicant must stand naked under the full moon. Then she crouched and unwrapped the knife, letting it rest on the silk while she rose. Wiping the third finger of her left hand with the alcohol sponge, she jabbed the point of the lancet into her fingertip, again crouching while three bright beads of her blood dropped onto the athame's handle. Immediately, she pressed the cotton ball to her fingers. No more of her blood must be allowed to fall.

When she was sure the bleeding had stopped, she discarded the cotton and reached for the athame. No sign of blood stained the hilt as it nestled into her palm—it was as though the athame had absorbed her blood. With her bare feet planted firmly on the earth, she raised the knife point upward in both hands, staring into the cold light of the moon.

Words welled up in her, flowing from her lips as though spoken by someone else. "Great Mother," she intoned, "look upon your child with favor, for you are truly my only mother. Help me to always follow the right path, to do no unnecessary harm to any living being and to remember that I am but a part of the whole.

"Lend me moon-power, tonight of all nights, that I may confound our enemies, those who work against the greater good."

Moonlight glittered along the metal blade, flickering into her eyes until she was blinded by the silver glory of the moon. The athame vibrated in her hands, the tremor passing into her until her entire body was atremble with the power passing through the knife into her, seeping into every cell of her mind and body, changing her.

When her trembling ceased, she lowered the knife and plunged it hilt-deep into the ground, into the earth that nourishes all who live.

"May the power be sealed into this blade," she intoned, "ever ready to be renewed by the light of the full moon." Pulling the blade free, she once more raised the knife to the moon. "I promise never to use my athame for ill but always for good for as long as I live."

Unaware of the passage of time, her watch discarded with her clothes, Inary had no idea how long she felt compelled to stand holding the knife aloft in the moonlight. Only when she was freed from whatever spell gripped her did she become aware of her surroundings once again.

After rewrapping the knife in the silk, she donned her clothes, gathered up every scrap that told of her presence—lancet, cotton, alcohol wipe and the paper wrappings—and placed everything in her bag. As she slid the bag onto her shoulder, it came to her that she must hurry.

Unquestioningly, she rushed through the pines to her car and began backing along the overgrown track as fast as she dared while the need for haste beat through her with ever-increasing urgency. Finally reaching the highway, she swerved onto it and rammed down the accelerator.

Home, she must get home!

Suddenly, as clearly as though he sat beside her in the passenger seat, she heard Ford's voice.

Inary, he called. *Hear me, Inary!*

Alarmed by the desperation throbbing in his sending, she opened herself to him. *I hear you*, she told him wordlessly. *I hear you, Ford.*

Listen and obey, he commanded. *Save yourself. Don't come home!*

Ford! she called silently, then shouted his name aloud. "Ford!"

There was no answer.

CHAPTER FOURTEEN

With Ford's shout of *Don't come home!* echoing in her mind, Inary sped along the highway, trying unsuccessfully to get him to respond to her mental calling.

Though she hoped it might be because she wasn't yet skilled in this kind of communication, she knew in her heart of hearts that it was impossible for him to answer her because Ford was in danger, so terrible a danger that if she didn't reach him in time he'd die.

He'd urged her to save herself, but how could she ignore his peril? She was determined to find him and try with all her newly awakened powers to rescue him.

What did she have to combat an evil force? Would the moon-power of her athame be strong enough? She'd never tried to use the athame so she wasn't sure of her power; all she knew was that Ford was somewhere in her house and he was in desperate need of her help.

Despite flooring the accelerator, the miles seemed endless. Would she never get to Norwich? When she finally reached her turnoff, she barely slackened her speed, slewing her car into the turnoff leading to her drive. As she jounced over the uneven ground, she peered anxiously ahead, expecting to see the lights of her house. But there were no lights except for the moonlight. Why was her house in darkness?

Finally pulling up in front of the house, she screeched to a stop, flung herself from the car and raced toward the porch, halting abruptly when she heard a cat's high-pitched yowling. Ford had promised not to let her cats out after dark. Why had he?

The slither of claws on bark reached her ears and she looked up into the rowan. Gilgamesh perched on a limb high above her head, his eyes glowing in the moonlight. There was no sign of Enkidu. Although she'd expected danger, finding Gilgamesh in the rowan was additional proof that peril lurked nearby.

Warily, Inary reached into her bag, unwrapped the athame and, clutching it, advanced to the porch, half expecting to find the door unlocked. She was wrong— the door resisted when she tried to open it. Ramming the key into the lock, she turned it, but the door still refused to budge. Someone inside had shot the bolt. Ford? But why? She jammed her finger against the doorbell but no one came in answer to the repeated ringing.

Glancing up at Gilgamesh, who obviously had no intention of climbing down from the tree, she decided she'd have to try the back door, even though it was more than likely the shed had been bolted. As she hurried around the outside of the house, each and every shadow seemed to menace her, to offer potential peril. Her unease built and built until she found herself apprehensively inching along with her back against the house.

A sudden maniacal screech made her gasp in shock and freeze in position, waiting. Minutes passed. The frogs, those harmless callers of the night, silent for a time, began singing again, *"Knee-deep, knee-deep,"* as though all danger had passed. Taking heart, she'd begun to edge her way along the outside wall of the house when the piercing cry came again—three eerie, frightening notes.

All at once she reverted to being a small girl, sitting up in bed, sobbing in the night, terrified of the awful noise outside.

"It's only a bird, child," Aunt Inary had said. "Stop your sniffling."

She'd clung to her aunt, visions of birdlike monsters filling her mind.

"A small brown bird called a whippoorwill makes that loud call," her aunt had told her. "If you listen when he calls again, you can hear him say his name."

"Whippoorwill," Inary whispered to herself now. Of course. How foolish to let herself be spooked.

By the time she reached the shed, the bird had called twice more, each time from farther away. As she'd surmised, the shed door was bolted against her and she restrained her impulse to pound on the wood in anger and frustration. Why waste her time and energy when she was convinced no one would let her in no matter how hard and long she beat against the door?

She ran around to the front once again, finding that door still bolted. She glanced all about her. Gilgamesh had jumped from his tree limb onto the roof of the porch, where he stood looking down at her. Moonlight etched the outline of the pines sharply against the night sky and showed the barely leafed branches of the maples reaching upward like clutching fingers. Frogs croaked busily from the swamp. Nothing threatened her.

The danger was inside, she knew. With Ford. But how was she to get in to help him?

From his perch on the roof, the cat mewed plaintively at her. When she stared up at him, he padded over to the unlighted window of her bedroom and she recalled having opened it a crack this morning, the storm sash as well as the window. Had she ever closed either of them? She'd meant to but she didn't think she had.

Inary looked from the porch roof to the rowan tree where one branch nestled close to the house, almost touching the roof.

If I can climb up to that branch and it holds my weight, she told herself, I can reach the roof.

Since she dare not abandon the athame and she'd need both her hands to climb, she retrieved the silk wrapping from her bag, tied the knife into it and then secured the silk around her waist. She reached the lowest limb of the rowan by jumping up, clutching it and then swinging herself onto the branch. The next branch that looked sturdy enough to bear her was almost out of reach. Struggling to pull herself up to it, she scraped her hands on the bark before gaining her goal.

Just above her head was the branch that would take her to the porch roof. Unfortunately, it formed a Y a few feet from the trunk, and the one she must use was the smaller of the two separated limbs. Climbing up, she straddled the roof branch and began to inch her way along. The wood creaked ominously, bending beneath her weight, the far end of the limb drooping until it rested on the roof.

Her legs bumped against the roof edge and she teetered dangerously until in desperation she flung herself forward, fingers scrabbling on the shingles as she searched for handholds. The branch sprang back. She lay flat on her stomach on the roof with her feet dangling precariously in space. Digging her fingernails into the spongy old shingles, she gingerly drew up her legs until she was kneeling. Then she began to crawl up the steep pitch of the roof toward her bedroom windows, where the cat waited.

At last reaching them, she felt for the bottom edge of the farthest storm window to her right. Unlatched! She pulled it toward her and, as it opened, Gilgamesh leapt past her. When he disappeared into the dark room, she knew someone had raised the inside window far higher than the no-more-than-an-inch opening she'd left. Boldly she thrust one foot inside and, meeting no resistance, squirmed through the narrow opening of the storm sash and eased down until she sat on the sill with one leg inside her bedroom.

Finding the inner window had been raised as high as it would go, she slid the rest of the way into the room. Huddled on the floor, aware she'd made a bit of noise climbing inside, she listened for any sound, any indication someone had heard and was coming to investigate.

Deciding she was safe so far, she rose, felt for and found the light switch. But when she flicked it, the room remained in darkness. Either the bulbs had burned out or, as she strongly suspected, someone had pulled the main switch to cut off the electricity to the entire house. For what malevolent purpose? she wondered.

Gilgamesh pressed against her ankle, briefly startling her until she realized what she felt. Reaching down to touch him, she discovered his fur was raised.

I don't like it, either, she told him silently. Something's terribly wrong.

She stared into the darkness of the hall, fancying the house hummed around her, an eerie sensation she couldn't account for. Where was Ford? She opened her mouth to call his name and held. No. It might be fatal to call attention to the fact that she'd managed to get inside.

Untying the silk from around her waist, she removed the athame, grasping the hilt firmly in her hand. Instantly a picture of the pentacle formed in her mind, the pentacle with a shadowy figure inside the circled star. Inary drew in her breath. Ford? Why would he do such a dangerous thing? And how could he have gotten inside the locked room?

Like a light flooding her mind, it came to her what she'd forgotten, what she now knew Roy had hypnotized her into forgetting. Panic-stricken by what had happened to her in the locked room a week or so ago, she'd relocked it and, in revulsion, flung the key down the attic stairs. She hadn't noticed where the key landed and had temporarily forgotten her impulsive rejection of the key.

Now she realized it must have bounced down to land on the stairs to the main floor, probably wedging itself between the carpet runner and the wood of a step, making the key difficult to see. But when Roy was here he'd found it. She'd even watched him pick up the key, though she hadn't realized what he was doing.

And then he'd made her forget what she'd seen, made her forget the key entirely. Therefore it must be Roy, not Ford, who'd unlocked the door in the attic. Roy was in her house! Had he climbed in through her bedroom window? If so, he must have surprised Ford, who believed the house was safely secured. It was her fault the window had been left open.

Afraid but determined, Inary left her bedroom. When the hall switch also failed to turn on a light, she felt her way along the dark hall to the attic door, shuddering when she found it open. Carefully, cautiously, she climbed the stairs, sensing Gilgamesh beside her. When she reached the attic, she saw, by the moonlight slanting through the skylight, Enkidu stationed outside the locked door. But was it really locked?

Gathering her fading courage, she crossed to the door and tried the knob. It *was* locked.

She closed her eyes, gripping the athame hilt tightly. Inside her closed lids a picture formed of what was beyond the door. Three candles flickered in the points of the pentacle, but the room was also bright with moonlight because the torn black blind had been ripped entirely away from the window. Inside the pentacle, as she'd seen before, a man crouched. It was Roy, she saw now, dressed in black. Another man lay unmoving on the floor outside the circle. She drew in her breath. Ford. Was he alive? He had to be! She must reach him. But how?

When her inner vision showed her that the key to the door was in the lock on the inner side, it came to her what she must do and she opened her eyes. Without hesitation, she touched the point of the athame to the lock. Holding it there, she visualized the key on the inside turning and unlocking the door. Hearing the click, she pulled back the knife and reached for the knob. Enkidu hissed. Behind her, Gilgamesh growled low in his throat.

As silently as she could, Inary eased open the door. The cats backed away, retreating to the far side of the attic. The hum she'd sensed earlier emanated from this room. She found it stronger here, distorting her thoughts and forcing her to push her way into the room as though the hum had somehow thickened the air. It seemed to her as she struggled to reach Ford that the humming rose around Roy inside the pentacle, making an almost visible pattern to accompany his chant.

Focusing on Ford, she saw to her horror that a cloud of darkness, apparent nowhere else in the room, hovered over him, a darkness that made her skin prickle with dread. She feared death lay within that darkness.

Try as she might to fight her way toward Ford, the athame tugged her in another direction, toward the circle enclosing the pentacle. Toward Roy.

When she reached the circle she found herself up against an invisible but impenetrable barrier and recalled what she'd read in the grimoire: "The one within the pentacle casts a protective spell about himself to protect against the dark force he calls up outside the magic circle. While the one within may leave the pentacle at will, nothing and no one from the outside may enter, thus keeping him safe from harm. The exception is a fully powered athame, which can rend the barrier if its power be used for good, the intent of the adept wielding it being to combat evil."

As if by its own will, her athame lifted in her hand, making her force its point against the unseen barrier. To her surprise, the athame cleaved through and she found herself inside the circle, face-to-face with Roy. He stopped chanting, his blue eyes glittering angrily.

Lifting the athame as a shield between them, she said coldly, "Enough! You're not welcome in my house. Leave. Immediately."

Roy shifted his gaze to the athame and kept it there. "I'll leave," he said, "only if you force me from this room, step by step. By then, what I've called up will have succeeded in sucking away Werlich's life force. Werlich is almost gone as it is. A few more moments and he'll be dead. Is that what you want?"

Inary glanced quickly at Ford, and her heart sank when she saw that the darkness had dipped down to cover his head. She rushed from the circle and dropped to her knees beside him, praying she'd be in time. Reaching through the dark force, she pressed the flat of the athame's blade against Ford's forehead. An icy chill penetrated her hand but she persisted, even though she felt as though the flesh and bones of her hand and arm were freezing solid.

Gradually the darkness thinned, dispersing as it lifted away from Ford. At the same time she heard him moan, she noticed that the athame's blade no longer gleamed, but had turned dark and lifeless.

I've used up the moon-power, she thought in dismay.

But with it she'd saved Ford, and that meant more to her than the loss of power, more than anything else in the world.

Roy's chant swelled from the pentacle to fill the room once more with the insidious humming, a humming that beckoned to her, luring her toward the magic circle enclosing Roy. Inary resisted, fighting the impulse, but it was irresistible. Stumbling to her feet, she was drawn, step by step, toward Roy. Inside the points of the pentacle, the flames of the three black candles burned fiercely.

Roy smiled, a malevolent flaring of his lips, as he pointed toward the barrier, making a sign with his fingers that seemed to temporarily set aside the protective spell and allow her to enter because the humming whirled her through and cast her at Roy's feet.

Though sensation had returned to the hand that held the athame, Inary could no longer feel power in the knife; it was as lifeless as its dull blade. Without the use of the athame, she was convinced she was helpless, and as though to confirm it, she found herself unable to move.

Roy gazed down at her. "My power is greater than yours and Werlich's combined," he boasted. "I control you completely. Together you and I will call up a demonic force to do my bidding, a force that—"

"No!" she cried. "I won't help you!"

"You have no choice. When I begin the incantation, you will repeat each word after me—*Bagabi.*" He paused, waiting.

Inary remembered the word as one she'd intoned when she'd had her terrible vision in this same pentacle. To her horror, she found herself shaping the hideous syllables. *"Bagabi,"* she whispered.

Your power wanes because you've lost belief. Aunt Inary's voice spoke in her head. *Believe in your power and it will be there. You can move if you so will.*

Believe. How often she'd heard that word from Ford, and now her aunt repeated it.

"Laca," Roy chanted.

Feeling the word forming obscenely in her throat, Inary clamped her lips together, closed her eyes and visualized the glade where she'd stood naked under the moon with power pouring into her, filling her.

I still have that power, she told herself fiercely. I believe it. I can and I will move. *Now.*

Opening her eyes, she sprang to her feet and burst free of the circle, hurrying to Ford, who was trying to sit up. She helped him rise, and as she touched him, a tingle ran up her arm from the hand holding the athame and she saw the blade begin to lose its dullness. Ignoring Roy's chanting and the horrible humming, she concentrated on getting herself and Ford out of this hellish room.

They'd almost reached the door when the humming changed to a triumphant roar. Glancing apprehensively over her shoulder, Inary saw, next to the pentacle, a whirling spiral of darkness shot through with crimson flames. Inside the circle, Roy pointed at her. She lunged for the door, but before she touched the knob she was drawn against her will into the vortex of the spiral, overwhelmed, gagged by noisome odors, embraced by evil and surrounded by darkness.

The room faded from her vision, she was spinning, spinning horribly, spinning away into nothingness.

Words formed faintly in her dazed mind. Words from Ford. *No one can control you. Nothing can control you. Free yourself.*

Ford believed in her. In the whirling chaos holding her prisoner, she struggled grimly to hold to her own belief in her newly discovered power.

Exerting all her will, she raised the athame up, up until it was over her head. "Go back," she bade the whirling darkness, forcing the words from her lips:

"Return to whence you came,

"Return without strength,

"Return without name."

Without warning, she found herself sprawled on the floor in the pentacle room, no longer a part of the deadly spiral. Ford bent to her, lifting her to her feet.

The malevolent force called up by Roy had vanished, though the candles still burned and Roy himself still crouched in the pentacle. Oddly, his head was bowed and he had his hands crossed over his head as though trying to ward off something, making her wonder fleetingly what it could be, since the circle protected him. Didn't it? Or had the rending with the athame somehow weakened the barrier?

Outside the closed door, she could hear the cats yowling. She didn't resist when Ford flung the door open and propelled her from the room; she was only too glad to leave that evil place. On the other hand...

"Roy's still inside the magic circle," she reminded Ford. "He hasn't yet been defeated."

"I'm getting us and the cats out of this house," Ford insisted as he locked the door to the pentacle room and pocketed the key. "While we still *can* get out."

With the cats dashing ahead of them, they hurried down the attic stairs and had reached the darkness of the second floor hall when the laughter began, a mindless and dreadful, altogether inhuman laughter. Inary shuddered and clutched Ford's arm tighter.

"As I feared," he muttered. "The dark force—"

His words were cut off by a loud crash from the attic. Ford shoved Inary in the direction of the stairs to the first floor. "Run!" he ordered. "Get in your car and drive like hell."

"Not without you," she cried.

And then it was too late to make a choice.

CHAPTER FIFTEEN

"Run, damn it!" Ford shouted at Inary for the second time as he tried to shove her toward the stairs leading to the first floor. "I'll hold him off."

The unearthly laughter grew louder as she shook her head, determined to stand beside Ford no matter what. A dark figure suddenly loomed at the foot of the attic stairs, a man's figure.

At least we're facing Roy, Inary thought in some relief, something human rather than those horrors in the attic. Ford has bested Roy before—chances are he will again. But she was unnerved by the continuing laughter as Roy rushed toward them along the darkened corridor.

Brushing past her with such force she staggered into the wall, Roy lunged at Ford. In the dim moonlight filtering into the hall from her bedroom windows, she watched in stunned disbelief as Roy hoisted Ford over his head. Impossible! Ford was heavier than Roy, certainly too heavy for the slighter man to lift so effortlessly. Ford wrenched himself free, stumbling as he landed, then falling. She gasped as, unable to regain his footing, Ford tumbled down the stairs.

When Ford failed to reappear, Roy turned to her and she recoiled from his gleaming red eyes. Another impossibility. Frightened by what she saw, Inary backed away, retreating into her bedroom. There, in the silvery light, she stared at the man who threatened her. Though he had Roy's shape and appearance, she realized he wasn't entirely human. Not anymore. Hair rose on her nape. What was he?

She shut away her agonized worry over how badly injured Ford might be, fully aware she needed all her wits about her if either she or Ford were to survive.

The dulled blade of the athame had regained some of its gleam, but, she feared, not enough to counter whatever Roy had become, though she meant to use the knife if she got the chance.

For an instant she thought she smelled smoke, but then all other scents were swamped by a fetid, foul odor—the same miasma given off by the dark force in the attic—and she realized the stench came from Roy. That dreadful darkness had entered and possessed him.

He sprang at her and she tried to twist away from him, but he moved too fast for her to escape. Caught off balance, she fell so hard against the footboard of the bed that the athame was jarred loose from her grip, falling onto the bed. Before she could attempt to retrieve the knife, he yanked her to her feet, hauled her against him and brought his mouth down on hers.

Bile rose in her throat as she understood he intended to rape her first. She struggled in vain to free herself. Even as a man he'd been stronger than she, and now his strength was inhuman. As he bore her to the floor, she decided her only hope was to use her newly acquired power against him. If she could without the athame in her hand.

Gather it, shape the power as a weapon, then strike. No one spoke the words in her mind; they arose from deep within her. As she sought to obey, she tried to ignore Roy's loathsome caresses.

She felt her power coiled within her, waiting. Using the coiled image, she visualized a striking snake and flung her power serpent at Roy. He grunted, his grip loosening. She rolled away and leapt to her feet, only to find herself trapped between the bed and the windows.

When she tried to scramble across the bed to get past him and reach the door, he flung himself over the footboard and pinned her to the mattress. Though she could feel the athame beneath her hip, she couldn't reach for it because he'd forced her arms above her head and grasped both her wrists in one of his hands. Instead of struggling, she used the coil again, imagining a noose of power slipping over his head and tightening around his neck.

Gagging, Roy released her hands to grope at his throat. Seizing her chance, Inary pulled the athame free and thrust the flat of the blade against his body. He reared back, but as she slid off the bed to run past him, he caught her arm, pulling her hard against him. His red eyes gazed malevolently into hers, sapping her will, making her power slip from her grasp.

No. She shouted the word silently.

He laughed, a chilling, alien sound that slithered unpleasantly into her ears, further draining her of strength. He forced her back, back, against the bed, and though she still gripped the athame in one hand, its blade had dulled once more, making the knife useless. Except as the dagger it resembled.

The athame must never be used to draw blood, to kill by penetration.

A warning from the grimoire. What was she to do? Before she could decide, Roy flung her onto the bed and dropped heavily on top of her, his weight half suffocating her as he pawed at her clothes.

Words ran together in her head—was he chanting? *Someone* was.

"Time goes in
"Time goes out
"The darkness within
"Shall be cast out."

Roy growled, swinging away from her to leap into the air and land, crouching, to face the man standing in the doorway. Ford!

Without waiting to see what would happen, Inary flung herself across the bed to the open window and thrust the athame through the opening into the moonlight, sending up a voiceless plea for aid against the evil within the room. The moon's silver rays caressed the blade, making it shimmer.

When she dared to stop concentrating on repowering the knife, Inary glanced over her shoulder. To her dismay, she saw Ford on the floor, Roy astride him, his hands gripping Ford's neck, choking him.

A surge of power ran along the athame, pouring into her. She whirled away from the window. Coming up behind Roy, she pressed the flat of the blade to the back of his neck, at the same time summoning up her own power and directing it through the athame. For a moment nothing happened. Then Roy convulsed, his body twisting in a massive spasm that flung him off Ford and onto the floor where he writhed hideously.

Inary dropped to her knees beside Ford, who was gasping for breath. She helped him sit up and together they watched as darkness first enveloped Roy's convulsing body, then lifted and dissipated. As the dark cloud vanished, Roy went limp and lay unmoving.

Only then did Inary realize the bedroom was filling with smoke. Real smoke, not something called up from within a pentacle. "The candles!" she cried, jumping up.

"The attic's on fire," Ford said hoarsely, struggling to his feet. He staggered across to Roy and knelt to feel along the downed man's jaw for the carotid pulse. "Nothing," he told her after a moment. "He's dead."

Seeing Ford meant to drag the body down the stairs, she started to help him, but he shook his head, saying, "I'll manage. You call the Norwich Fire Department."

To Inary's relief, the cats were downstairs, crowding close to her feet as she punched in the emergency fire number.

Minutes later, she, Ford and the cats were gathered outside, a short distance from where Roy's body lay covered with an afghan hastily snatched from the couch.

Inary tore her gaze away from the flames beginning to lick through the roof and looked at Ford. "I killed Roy," she said, her voice quivering. "I killed him with the athame."

Ford put an arm around her shoulders, drawing her closer to him. "Nuhaim doomed himself," he said, "when he called up that dark force, a damned dangerous business. When you thrust the force away from you, it waited, biding its time, and then turned on and possessed him the moment he stepped out of the pentacle. Because he could no longer see or sense it, he thought the force was gone.''

Inary shuddered. "But my athame..."

"Your athame didn't kill him. What your athame plus your power did was make the dark force leave Roy. I believe the shock of the possession itself caused his death. He was a walking dead man from the moment the force took control of him.''

Inary felt somewhat consoled, knowing Ford wouldn't lie to her. Leaning her head against his shoulder, she said, "I was so afraid you'd been killed when you fell down the stairs."

"If Nuhaim had thrown me down as he intended to, I might well *have* been killed. While I don't recommend tumbling down—the fall did knock me out for a few minutes—I managed to survive."

Hearing the rise and fall of a distant siren, she straightened and said, "What are we going to tell the firemen?"

"We'll say that, unknown to either of us, Nuhaim went into the attic and somehow set the place afire—which is the truth. We can't tell them what he died from because we don't know—also true." He dropped his arm from her shoulders and bent to pick up Enkidu. "Bring Gilgamesh to your car. We'll drive it to my place to get the car and the cats out of the way."

Once the cats were inside Ford's house, he insisted she stay with them while he waited by the drive for the fire trucks.

"Here's where we mix a bit of creative lying in with the truth," he said. "You arrived home from your hospital shift after midnight and noticed an upstairs window was open. Fearing someone had broken into your house, you came here and woke me. By the time

I got dressed and went with you to your place, smoke was drifting from the open window. We entered the house and you rescued the cats while I investigated.

"I found Nuhaim's body on the attic stairs and dragged him outside while you called the fire department. You were so upset by the ordeal that, acting as your doctor, I gave you a sedative and ordered you to bed at my house."

"But—"

"There's no time to argue, the trucks are almost here. Stay put." He turned and strode from the house.

When Inary tried to watch what was going on from the windows, she discovered the trees blocked her view of the fire. Sighing, she sat on the couch, where both cats joined her.

She couldn't object to the way Ford had stretched the truth. If they tried to tell the real truth they'd either be accused of lying or suspected of belonging in Sweetgrass as patients rather than employees. And she supposed Ford's story was strengthened by presenting her as a fragile little woman, needing protection.

"But I'm not fragile," she told the cats. "I no longer need anyone's protection."

Gilgamesh favored her with his most scathing green glare.

"Oh, all right, maybe yours," she muttered.

She *was* exhausted, though. This Walpurgis Night had been a gruesome horror, the worst experience of her life. She was so depleted that she didn't even have the energy to worry over the fire's outcome. Leaning her head against the back of the couch, she closed her eyes....

She floated effortlessly, buoyed up by unknown forces, drifting without fear until at last she settled into a haven where gentle hands stripped away what she wore and wrapped her in a warm cocoon of safety. Here, nothing could harm her. Even though aware she was capable of protecting herself, she gratefully accepted the gift of another's protection, nestling into the wonderful warmth and relaxing in complete trust.

Time passed. Whether hours or minutes, she didn't know. Hovering languorously between sleeping and waking, she found herself still cuddled up to warmth, but an unyielding warmth, not a soft cocoon....

Inary opened her eyes to the dim light of predawn. On the pillow above her head, a cat purred reassuringly, yet she knew she wasn't in her own bed. Wearing only her bra and panties, she was lying spoon fashion, curled against a man's bare back. Ford's back. She was in Ford's house, in his bed. And he was asleep.

Pushing all the questions and all the frightening past from her mind, Inary smiled. She was exactly where she wanted to be, under the right circumstances. Answers could wait, coming to terms with past events could wait, everything else could wait. She'd finally gotten her turn to be in charge.

Leave us, she told the cats wordlessly, and waited until she heard one, then the second, thump that told her they'd jumped off the bed.

Ford stirred, turning onto his back as she edged away to allow him room. Without opening his eyes, he sighed and settled into sleep once again.

Perfect, she told herself, feeling a coil of power build within her as she gazed at the sleeping Ford—purely feminine power, nothing to do with witchcraft.

Reaching carefully, she folded the covers away from him until his body was exposed to the waist. Using the tips of her fingers, she lightly traced a concentric circle around one of his nipples, homing in at last to rub the nipple delicately. When she repeated the caress with the other nipple, he murmured something under his breath, words she didn't catch. When he didn't waken, she decided he must be talking in his sleep.

Raising herself, she brought her lips and tongue to his nipple, making him shift his hips and groan. Unhooking her bra, she shrugged out of it and leaned over to rub her bared breasts against his chest, the stimulating rasp of his chest hair on her nipples peaking them and sending a hot, tingling message of need throughout her body.

Her heart pounded as she folded the covers down and down, until her breath caught at what she saw. Unlike her, Ford was naked and clearly showed the effect of her caresses. Heat flared deep within her as she viewed the pleasing result of what she was doing to him.

Her fingertips brushed gently against his arousal, discovering first the velvet texture and then the hard need, fueling her own desire until she ached with wanting.

Sliding off her panties, she rose up until she straddled him and then, just as his eyes opened, she eased down over him, taking him in, taking him where he belonged.

His arms closed around her convulsively, pulling her hard against him as he thrust up. She cried out from the intense shock of pleasure of their coming together but also in thrilled surprise at the sudden surge of sensation flowing from him now that he was awake.

Holding her to him, he rolled them both over until she was beneath him. Her hips began to move involuntarily, finding a counterpart rhythm to his thrusts, and all the while her own excited wonder mingled with his. She felt his rapture along with her own, until the sensations became so intermingled she couldn't tell his pleasure from hers.

The joining of their minds as well as their bodies surpassed anything she'd ever imagined. They were truly together, truly one as they reached for and found the ultimate joy.

When they lay side by side with Ford still holding her, he murmured, "I'm not complaining, but wasn't that a trifle rash?"

She put a hand over his mouth. "Stop being a shrink. You enjoyed being seduced, admit it."

"There's no doubt that's a secret male fantasy and I'm no exception. What you did to me was a dream come true." He ran his thumb over her nipple, and she felt an anticipatory tingle. "But it sure shot to hell all my plans to go slow and easy. And then there's the issue of you possibly having diminished your newly awakened powers. To say nothing of birth control—I know damn well you're not protected and you didn't give me a chance to use anything."

"See?" she accused.

"See what?"

"If I'd waited for you to initiate things you'd have analyzed the whole thing to death before we even got started. Making love with you didn't affect my power—couldn't you tell?"

He drew her closer. "You know I could and did. Loving you was beyond anything I ever believed I'd experience." He smiled."I freely admit I can't wait to try it again."

"So what are you waiting for? Didn't anyone ever tell you that female witches don't conceive unless they choose to?"

"I thought that was some old wives' tale."

She shook her head. "The grimoire says it's true. And, besides, I can feel within myself that it is."

His hand slid caressingly over her hip. "We take it slow and easy, this time. Remember, you're not the only witch in this bed." He bent his head to her breast.

Inary gasped in delight, and his disturbingly erotic caresses soon made her realize it was equally blissful to be seduced.

When Inary and Ford finally drifted back to reality once more, both cats jumped onto the bed and climbed onto them to stare into their faces and complain loudly.

"They don't approve of what we're doing?" Ford asked.

"It's plain you have a lot to learn about cats," she said. "They've already accepted us as a couple. Their message is far more urgent—they want to go out. Which means at least one of us has to get up."

In the end they both did. Much later, after they finally got dressed and fed both the cats and themselves, Inary and Ford walked over to view the fire damage to her house.

"The attic's gone," Inary said. "Burned completely away. That means the pentacle's gone as well."

Ford nodded. "The fire chief thought the destruction was confined to the attic and the roof. He warned there'd be some water damage to the upstairs but he thought you ought to be able to rebuild."

Inary stared at the house, considering. "Last night I was hoping it would all burn," she said slowly. "But I feel differently now that I know the pentacle has been destroyed forever. That was the only evil in the house."

"Yes, the house has been cleansed. The insurance should cover rebuilding."

"You don't sound enthusiastic."

"We don't need two houses."

"Oh?"

"You mean you refuse to marry me?"

She lifted an eyebrow. "I was never asked."

He pulled her into his arms, touched his forehead to hers, and the outpouring of his emotions overwhelmed her—love, desire, respect, need...all for her. "Marry me," he whispered. "It must be obvious that I can't get along without you."

She opened to him, letting him know without words how much she loved and needed him, and then she murmured, "Yes, we'll get married as soon as possible."

"And then we'll figure out what to do with two houses," he said before he kissed her.

Walking back to his house, she said, "You didn't mention Roy."

"We'll have to make a statement to the sheriff, but I don't anticipate any problem. Nuhaim's reputation locally isn't good—the fire chief mentioned that he'd heard Nuhaim had been involved in some kind of 'weird cult,' to quote him."

Inary shuddered. "I wish there'd never be another Walpurgis Night."

"With the pentacle gone, we won't be bothered again. And, whatever happens, we'll be together." He stopped and kissed her. "And damn near invincible, the two of us."

When they resumed walking, she said, "We can try to help Mouse now. And if we do, maybe—"

"Maybe we can adopt her. I hope so. She needs us."

"Don't you imagine there are other children we could help?"

He nodded. "We'll try to find them."

Linking her hand with his, she smiled, the two of them in perfect communication.

They'd almost reached the house when Enkidu appeared from between the trees, heading their way. Inary halted, staring at the cat trailing him. "That's not Gilgamesh," she said, frowning.

"No, it appears to be tailless—a Manx—for one thing, a tabby, for another, and thirdly, *she* seems to be carrying a kitten in her mouth."

"That's Tansy!" Inary cried. "That's my aunt's cat!"

Gilgamesh brought up the rear, shepherding the other two cats ahead of him until all three halted beside Ford and Inary, who crouched to welcome the newcomers. Without protest, Tansy released the tiny tabby kitten into Inary's hands, watching anxiously as Inary examined it.

"A female," she told Ford. "My aunt often said, though it wasn't necessarily typical of the breed, her Manx cats never had more than one kitten and always a female." She stroked the mother cat behind her ears, murmuring to her, calling her by name.

Tansy responded by rubbing against Inary's leg.

"I'm so excited," Inary said rising, cupping the kitten carefully. "Isn't it wonderful that Tansy's alive and well and has come home with her daughter?"

"It's interesting she waited until the pentacle was destroyed."

Inary stared at him. "I hadn't considered that."

Ford shrugged. "Cats have unusual instincts—I don't pretend to understand them. I have a hunch that Gilgamesh and Enkidu knew all along where Tansy and her kitten were, and once they knew it was safe, they promptly trotted off to fetch the two, and now they've brought their prospective wives home."

"Prospective wives?" Inary began to laugh. "You're absolutely right. Gilgamesh has never been the kind to let me get away with having all the fun!"

*　*　*　*　*

And now from Silhouette Shadows
an exciting preview of

A Silence of Dreams
by Barbara Faith

CHAPTER ONE

It was raining the afternoon Nicky Fairchild left Milan, and it was still raining a few hours later when the train pulled into the Venice railway station.

When the train lurched to a stop, she put on her leather jacket and smoothed her flyaway blond hair under the red plaid cap she'd picked up at a street fair in London. Hefting her backpack, she followed the other passengers down the aisle of the train to the door, and through the terminal to the exit.

And there it was. Venice, the dream city she had so longed to see, a shimmery illusion through the slanting gray rain. Exotic, romantic, implausible Venice. She stood on the steps of the train station watching the gondolas glide by.

Crowds jostled about her, but she stood, mesmerized by the sight of the most fantastic of cities.

She sneezed, hoping her cold wouldn't last very long, and stepped out into the rain, in search of the Pensione Villa Lucia, which a backpacker she'd met in Paris had told her about.

The lobby of the Pensione Villa Lucia was small and shabbily Romanesque. Red velvet tassled drapes hung from tall windows. Overstuffed velvet furniture graced marble floors. No one was in the lobby, but there was a hand bell on the carved-mahogany reception desk.

She called a tentative, "Hello?" and when there was no answer, tapped the bell with the palm of her hand.

"*Si, si,* I am coming." A woman came hurrying into the lobby from one of the corridors. "Can I help you? You are looking for a room?" she asked.

Nicky eased the backpack off her shoulders. "Yes, if you have one."

"*Si,* I have. This is not the tourist time so we are not busy," the signora said. "I have a nice room on the second floor. Come, I show you."

Nicky followed the signora up a wide winding staircase. The carpeting was worn, but the carved dark bannister was finely polished and beautiful. The corridor was dark, and so was the room the signora motioned her to enter.

"*Momento,*" the signora said, then crossed the floor and threw open the wooden shutters.

And there was Venice, with all its sounds and smells and vibrant life. It didn't matter that the once-elegant carpet in the room had faded, or that the pink-and-lavender-flowered wallpaper was peeling. Nicky hurried to the window and leaned out. From below came the shouts of the gondoliers and the splash of water from a passing vaporetto, a water bus. A flat barge-like boat had pulled up to the dock to unload cases of beer. The man unloading looked up and saw her leaning out of the window.

"*Buon giorno,*" he called up to her.

"*Buon giorno,*" she called back, and with a smile she turned to the signora. "It's wonderful," she said. "I'll take it."

"*Bene!*" The signora held out her hand. "I am the Signora Brendisi." She handed Nicky a key. "*Ben venuto,* welcome. How long will you stay?"

"I'm not sure." Nicky sneezed. "A week. Maybe two."

"As long as you like." A look of concern crossed her face. "You have a cold, yes?"

Nicky nodded. "I picked it up in Paris."

"You must take care."

"I will. *Grazie.*"

By morning Nicky was burning with fever. Her throat was worse and her chest felt like an elephant was sitting on it. She dragged herself out of bed and made it to the alcove of the kitchen for breakfast. Signora Brendisi served her hot tea with lemon, a hard roll and a concerned look.

"It is better you stay in today," she said.

Nicky shook her head. "I have to go to American Express," she croaked. "I'm waiting for a letter." She summoned a smile. "I won't be gone long, but I really do have to go."

By the time she returned to the pensione she was shaking with chills and fever, so dizzy she could barely stand. She went to bed and stayed there all day. The next morning she was too ill to get up for breakfast. When the maid came at noon to make up her room, she said something too quickly in Italian for Nicky to understand and went scurrying out the door.

A few minutes later Signora Brendisi appeared. "You are *malato*?" she asked. "Sick, yes?"

"It's just a bad cold," Nicky managed to whisper.

The signora put a hand on Nicky's forehead. "*Dio mio,* you are burning with fever. We must call a doctor at once. My friend, Dr. Raviggia, is a neighbor. I will telephone him."

"No!" Nicky struggled to a sitting position. The room tilted, and she slid back down under the blanket. "I'll feel better tomorrow. Please don't call a doctor. I can't afford..."

But the Signora Brendisi had already hurried out of the room. Five minutes later she returned. "Dr. Raviggia is not in Venice," she said. "He has gone to Roma to visit his mother. But he has a houseguest, a doctor, too, a specialist in the heart who is here in Venice to teach for a few weeks. I have left a message for him. The housekeeper assures me he will come as soon as possible."

"I only have a cold," Nicky started to protest. "I don't need..." But it was too much effort to speak. She closed her eyes, and as she drifted to sleep, she wondered how much a heart surgeon charged for telling a patient to take two aspirins and go to bed....

"Signorina?"

Nicky opened her eyes and looked up at the man bending over her. Mephistopheles with dark Mediterranean features. A curl of dark hair hanging down over a broad forehead. A forbidding frown curving a sensuously cruel mouth. A questioning intensity in his pale green eyes.

He put a cold hand on her forehead, and she winced. "I am Dr. Carlo Santini," he said in accented English. "How do you feel?"

"Not great," she whispered.

He opened the top few buttons of her nightgown and put a stethoscope on her bare chest. "Take a deep breath," he said.

She tried to, but all that came out was a wheezing cough.

The frown deepened. He raised her to a sitting position and eased the cold stethoscope down her back. "Again," he said. "A deep breath." He laid her back down and put a thermometer under her arm. It, too, was cold.

"What is your name?" he asked.

"Nicky...Nicolina Fairchild."

He took the thermometer from under her arm and looked at it with a deepening frown. "You have pneumonia, signorina," he said. "You must go to the hospital."

"Can't," she said.

He bent over Nicky, and suddenly she found herself being wrapped in the blanket that covered her bed.

"Listen," she tried to say. "I don't want to go to a hospital. I can't—"

But he didn't listen. He simply bundled the blanket around her, picked her up and headed for the door. She tried to struggle, but he was bigger than she was. Six feet, probably. Football shoulders. Broad chest.

They were outside. The door closed behind them. Nicky felt rain on her face, then the blanket covered her and she couldn't see. She heard the sound of a motorboat, words shouted in Italian. Then she was on the boat, cradled in his arms.

Waves. The sharp stinging smell of the water, the coolness of the rain. And him. The beat of his heart against her cheek.

Nicky opened her eyes. The room was clean and white. She looked down at her arm and saw the needle there, the slow drip from the tube attached to the IV. Mephistopheles was sitting in a chair next to her bed.

"How are you?" he asked.

She wanted to say, You're the doctor, you tell me, but he didn't look as though he had much of a sense of humor, so she said, "Chest hurts."

He took the stethoscope from around his neck and turned her. She felt the coldness of metal on her back. When he eased her over she felt his hand on her forehead. Then the darkness came again, and she slept.

They had covered her head and shoulders with a plastic tent. She remembered the doctor had said she had pneumonia. Did people still die of pneumonia?

I never get sick, she wanted to tell somebody. Sniffles, maybe. The measles when she was seven and spending Christmas with her father. He had sat beside her bed. He'd read her stories and played games with her. She loved him, and when she was better and Christmas vacation was over, she wanted to stay with him.

"Maybe next year, when you're older," he'd said.

But by next Christmas he was dead. Her mother had been in Greece, and she had spent Christmas in a Connecticut boarding school.

If her father were here now...

She said, "Daddy?" and a hand grasped hers.

"Hang on," he said. "Fight!"

Nighttime again. Her breathing hard and rasping in the silence of the room. She drifted on the edge of consciousness, and every time she opened her eyes, he was there, his pale green eyes intense, serious, probing.

"Hard to breathe," she whispered.

He lifted the plastic and leaned down so that his face was close to hers. "You must try," he said. "You *must* get well. I won't lose you again!"

She looked at him, held by the intensity of his gaze. She felt the strength of the hand holding hers, pulling her back. Back from . . .

"You will get well," he said.

"Yes." Only a whisper. "Yes."

There were spring flowers in her room—lavender irises, daffodils and violets. Signora Brendisi came to visit and brought her a blue nightgown. "To match your eyes," she said.

She patted Nicky's hand. "Dr. Santini has assured me you are recovering, and that in a few days you will be out of the hospital and can return to the pensione. But you must rest when you do, yes?" Signora Brendisi smiled. "Dr. Santini is a good doctor. A little abrupt, perhaps, but nevertheless a good man. The nurses have told me that when you were so sick he rarely left your side."

"Yes, I remember. . . ." Pale green eyes gazing so intently into hers. And the words, *I won't lose you again.*

Again? What had he meant by that? She had never seen him before. . . .

**Relive the romance...
Harlequin and Silhouette
are proud to present**

A program of collections of three complete novels by the most
requested authors with the most requested themes. Be sure to
look for one volume each month with three complete novels by
top name authors.

In June: **NINE MONTHS** Penny Jordan
Stella Cameron
Janice Kaiser

**Three women pregnant and alone. But a lot can
happen in nine months!**

In July: **DADDY'S
HOME** Kristin James
Naomi Horton
Mary Lynn Baxter

**Daddy's Home...and his presence is long
overdue!**

In August: **FORGOTTEN
PAST** Barbara Kaye
Pamela Browning
Nancy Martin

**Do you dare to create a future if you've forgotten
the past?**

Available at your favorite retail outlet.

◈ HARLEQUIN®   ♥ Silhouette®

Take 4 bestselling love stories FREE

Plus get a FREE surprise gift!

Silhouette Books
is proud to present
our best authors,
their best books…
and the best in
your reading pleasure!

Throughout 1993, look for exciting
books by these top names in
contemporary romance:

DIANA PALMER—
Fire and Ice in June

ELIZABETH LOWELL—
Fever in July

CATHERINE COULTER—
Afterglow in August

LINDA HOWARD—
Come Lie With Me in September

When it comes to passion,
we wrote the book.

BOBT2

MEN · MADE IN AMERICA

Fifty red-blooded, white-hot, true-blue hunks from every State in the Union!

Beginning in May, look for MEN MADE IN AMERICA! Written by some of our most popular authors, these stories feature fifty of the strongest, sexiest men, each from a different state in the union!

Two titles available every other month at your favorite retail outlet.

In July, look for:

CALL IT DESTINY by Jayne Ann Krentz (Arizona)
ANOTHER KIND OF LOVE by Mary Lynn Baxter
(Arkansas)

In September, look for:

DECEPTIONS by Annette Broadrick (California)
STORMWALKER by Dallas Schulze (Colorado)

You won't be able to resist MEN MADE IN AMERICA!

SILHOUETTE® *Desire*

MAN OF
THE MONTH:
1993

They're tough, they're sexy...
and they know how to get the
job done....
Caution: They're

MEN AT WORK

Blue collar...white collar...these men are working overtime
to earn your love.

July:	Undercover agent Zeke Daniels in Annette Broadrick's ZEKE
August:	Aircraft executive Steven Ryker in Diana Palmer's NIGHT OF LOVE
September:	Entrepreneur Joshua Cameron in Ann Major's WILD HONEY
October:	Cowboy Jake Tallman in Cait London's THE SEDUCTION OF JAKE TALLMAN
November:	Rancher Tweed Brown in Lass Small's TWEED
December:	Engineer Mac McLachlan in BJ James's ANOTHER TIME, ANOTHER PLACE

Let these men make a direct deposit into your heart.
MEN AT WORK...only from Silhouette Desire!

MOM93JD